Rites and Witnesses

A Comedy

Rolando Hinojosa

Arte Público Press
Houston, Texas
1982

KLAIL CITY DEATH TRIP SERIES

Estampas del valle y otras obras
Klail City y sus alrededores
Korean Love Songs
Claros varones de Belken
Mi querido Rafa

Arte Público Press
University of Houston
Central Campus
Houston, Texas 77204-2090

Library of Congress Catalog No. 82-071655

Copyright © 1989 by Rolando Hinojosa

ISBN 0-934770-19-0

Second Printing, 1989

Printed in the United States of America

Trampled and mocked with many a loathed rite
Of lust and blood; he went unterrified,
Into the gulf of death;

Shelley

His means of death, his obscure burial,
No trophy, sword, nor hatchment o'er his bones,
No noble rite nor formal ostentation.

Shakespeare

In the mouth of two or three witnesses
shall every word be established

Corinthians xiii. 1

The Rites

1

"Who is he, Noddy?"

"His name's Jehú Malacara."

"And?"

"He's a local boy."

"I've never heard of him, Noddy."

"Yes, Noddy, neither have I. Who is he?"

"Well, Fredericka, he . . ."

"Don't *call* me that. Whenever you use . . ."

"Freddie, please. Go on, Noddy."

"Well, Junior, he's been working at the Savings and Loan for over a year now, and, ah, he's worked out very well."

"At the S. and L.? Who brought him?"

"Viola recommended him, Junior."

"I see."

"Viola Barragán?"

"Oh, well!"

"Go on, Freddie; you too, Ibby . . . She recommended him, and he's worked out very well."

"You've said that."

"And now, I suppose she wants him transferred here? That it?"

"No, Ibby; *I* want him here. As a loan officer he'd make a good assistant. Look: we need someone to help us on some of the up-coming land buys."

"We've never needed a Mexican before."

"We do now . . ."

"Oh, Noddy . . ."

"Which land buys, Noddy? Here in Belken?"

"Belken and Dellis County both, Junior."

"I see."

"What's Viola's stake in all of this?"

"She just wants to help him out, that's all."

"Ha!"

"Now, Fredericka . . ."

"Noddy!"

"Up to now we've never considered having a Mexican work at

the bank . . . Of course, if he's any good . . ."

"He is, Junior."

"Paying back favors, are you, Noddy?"

"Come on, Ibby, get off of that; you yourself know I'd already mentioned him to you way before this."

"Okay, from the top . . ."

"No need to: he already works for us at the S. and L., and I just want him over here, that's all. He's good. Sammie Jo knows him."

"She does?"

"From school, Freddie; they're about the same age."

"Well, maybe the Mexicans will be happy having one of their own working here."

"Are we being *pushed* into this?"

"No, not at all."

"What do we have at the Ranch? Three hundred families, is it?"

"Closer to five."

"Speaking of Mexicans, what about Javier Leguizamón? I'm sure he'd like one of his brood here . . ."

"In time . . ."

"Who *is* the boy, Noddy?"

"Like I said, his name's Malacara. He's a Klail High graduate, he joined the Army, later on he went up to Austin, the Army again for the Korean thing, the university again, and then he taught at Klail High for a couple of years . . ."

"What about the Leguizamóns?"

"Yes, and what's Viola's interest in this again?"

"She, ah, she wants him to get ahead, like I said. For God's sake, Freddie, he's just a kid!"

"Oh, I wasn't talking about *that*."

"And the Leguizamóns? Whatever else they are, they're a big voice in Mexican politics."

"It'll work it out."

"Do you know anything else about him, Noddy?"

"He's honest . . . he's a hard worker . . . he knows the area . . . *and* the people."

"And when are you planning to bring in this wonder boy of yours?"

"I'd like to start him next week, Freddie, but I wanted all of us to talk about it beforehand."

"*Is* there a problem, Noddy?"

"Not really."

"How much of a Not Really?"

"Ibby, it isn't a problem."

"What then?"

"Well, he may be related to the Buenrostro family."

"He's *what?*"

"To them?"

"Go on, Noddy."

"I think he's related to the Carmen Ranch Buenrostros, and . . ."

"Well! The Leguizamóns are really going to be tickled, won't they?"

"Polín Tapia says it isn't a blood kinship; that he was just raised there."

"Polín? Him? What does *he* know?"

"Just about everything, Freddie. Right, Ibby?"

"I'll say . . ."

"So he was raised there . . . at the Carmen Ranch."

"Off and on, Junior . . . from what I know, he's Sammie Jo's age, and that makes him the middle son's age, too."

"That would be Rafe, wouldn't it?"

"That's the one."

"How do you propose to smooth this out with Javier Leguizamón? I mean, the boy being raised in Quieto's land and all."

"It won't be that hard."

"Ha!"

"We're lucky: Jehú worked for Javier Leguizamón as a kid some 15 years ago, and Javier liked him. He watched him like a hawk, and . . ."

"And what?"

"And nothing, Ibby. Look: he'll probably be sharper than anything the Leguizamóns bring up."

"That's not even the *point,* Noddy."

"And, at the same time, we do Viola a good turn."

"What for?"

"Two things: future need and good business for now."

"Baloney!"

"Look, Freddie: I've met the kid, and he and I work well together. Okay? And let me tell you something: he's got the makings of a banker . . ."

"Ha!"

"It's true, Ibby; he *likes* banking."

"But if he's related to that family, the Leguizamóns are going to . . ."

"Freddie's right, you know."

"Well, Noddy?"

"I don't think I'll have any trouble, Junior . . . Viola can always talk to Javier, you know. There won't be any trouble."

"There *is* one problem, Noddy."

"Oh?"

"Where are you going to put him? I mean, will he be *out front?*"

"What Ibby is saying is that some of our Anglos won't like it . . ."

"The girls, you mean? Or is it Billy Markham?"

"The customers, Noddy."

"Well, I was planning to section off a part of the east wall and make that into a small office. Next to mine."

"It'll look bad with Billy not . . ."

"Jehú'll be the chief loan officer; he'll need an office."

"Junior, is that true?"

"Noddy, really now . . ."

"Look: he's the one who finally straightened out both the Anglo and Mexican poor risk loans at the S. and L. It was nothing but trouble for us, and now? He's good, I tell you."

"But what about Billy *Mark*ham? He's been here *four* years."

"And as dumb as his father. Look, if there's any trouble, we'll nudge Billy on over to the S. and L. . . . okay, Junior?"

"I think I'd like that."

"Is Jehú dark?"

"No, Freddie . . ."

"Well, I guess we've kicked this around long enough, and if you're satisfied, Noddy . . . It's okay with me. You do need some help. Ibby?"

"Fine with me, Freddie?"

"Oh, it's all right, I guess. I just hope you know what you're doing, Noddy."

"It'll work out, Freddie. A few years, maybe months, we'll put him up for County Commissioner . . . How's that?"

"Good enough . . . what's next?"

"Well, who's to replace the boy at the S. and L., then? Billy?"

"He could, I guess . . ."

"Look: let's move Billy out there; we'll just give him a bigger desk, and then we can farm the collecting end of it out. We have before, you know. It's a detail."

"Done. What's next?"

"It's the Osuna property, Junior."

"How's that coming along?"

"It's almost twelve, you all; can't it wait?"

"This won't take a minute, Freddie; look, I'll put Jehú . . ."

"How do you spell that anyway?"

"J-E-H-U."

"Oh, *Je*hu. That's Old Testament . . ."

"He's not one of the Jews, is he? Like the Leguizamóns?"

"Well, he's a Buenrostro . . ."

"But *is* he a Buenrostro? You said that Polín . . ."

"Let's not go off into that. You were saying, Noddy?"

"Yes; I'll put him on to the Osuna tract, and I'll oversee the preliminaries."

"What Osunas are those, you all? Are you talking about Osbaldo's property?"

"Ernesto's."

"Oh?"

"Give Freddie the outline, Noddy."

"Okay: Ibby and I have looked at that, ah, piece of property for quite a while now. It's good. Ah, I've had a good look at the will, the deeds, *and* the plats. It's a good buy."

"Don't tell me it's the Osuna land out in Edgerton?"

"No; that one's not for sale; it's part of the original grant, you know. Anyway, that land you're talking about spills on over to Dellis; by the gas plant. The one Ibby and I are talking about is river bottom land."

"Oh, I know which one you're talking about; it's the one just south of Bascom, by the Mexican cemetery."

"That's the one, Freddie."

"The Dellis County land is symbolic anyway, isn't it? I mean, original land grant and all that stuff?"

"Uh-huh; damn good, though."

"This one's just as good, isn't it?"

"Sure is."

"You see any trouble and smoke there?"

"Not yet . . ."

"You think the boy can handle it?"

"It'll be his first job, but he might as well start earning his money now as any time."

"Do we have anything else on tap for this morning? I'm starved."

"Well . . . there *is* one more thing. It's Family. It's about Sammie Jo and Sidney again . . ."

"Can't that wait until after lunch, Noddy?"

"I guess so . . . I'd like your advice on this, Freddie. Is two o'clock all right?"

"Two's fine . . . Oh, before I do go, you bringing in the boy this week?"

"A week from today; is that okay?"

"Good enough. See you all at two; I'll be at the Camelot."

"Bye, Freddie. You all?"

"Oh, let's have one of the girls bring something in . . . Junior?"

"No lunch for me, thanks . . . I'll see you all at two."

"Ibby?"

"Yeah, tell Esther to bring us something over to your office; we'll eat there."

"I'll buzz her."

And this, as Jehú Malacara was to learn, was how most Family matters were resolved. Three months later, Fredericka Blanchard was carted off with uterine cancer; she was then replaced, nominally as it turned out, by her brother, Sanford, who, among the Valley Mexicans was known as El Borrachín: Sanford the Drunk.

2

"Hi, how you doin'? I was told to wait here—with you; you know how long we got to wait?"

"I can't say . . . you okay?"

"What?"

"Are you okay? Are you doing all right?"

"Yeah . . . They just brought me in and sent me here. To you. But I'm okay; I'm one of the ones from Charlie Battery, the Two Nineteenth? Been here long?"

"Yeah, but we just set up this morning. We'll probably be moving on again."

"Yeah? Ah, where are you from?"

"The Two Nineteenth."

"No, I don't mean this shit, I mean where are you *from?* Back home?"

"Oh . . . I'm from Texas."

"No shit? I'm from Louisiana; yeah . . . and I've been to Beaumont, Houston, Galveston, Orange . . . all those places. You know where that is?"

"Yeah, that's up the coast from us; I'm from the Valley."

"Oh, yeah? Where's that?"

"That's way down there, by the border. Next to Mexico."

"Is that anywhere near El Paso?"

"No—we're a long way from there, too; we're near the Gulf, by the Rio Grande."

"Oh, yeah. That's way down there, isn't it? How far is that from Houston?"

"I don't really know; I guess it's about four hundred miles . . ."

"You been there? To Houston?"

"No . . ."

"Oh . . . It's a big town, Houston . . . Were you guys in the Pass? I mean, were you part of the bunch that got caught?"

"Sure, all of us were . . . you too."

"Yeah, but I was talking about the firing and the thermiting . . . Able Battery . . ."

"Yeah, that was us."

"Boy, you guys are fast. Was *he* with you?"

"Who you talking about?"

"The red-faced guy . . . you know, the sergeant who brought us in?"

"Yeah; he, ah . . ."

"Is he a friend of yours?"

"Yeah, he's . . ."

"How do you pronounce your name, anyway?"

"What's that?"

"Your name . . . how do you say it?"

"Oh. Buenrostro. Boo N Ross Troh. Buenrostro."

"Run together like that? . . . Spanish, right? My name's Ben Pardue, but they call me Rusty 'cause I'm from Ruston, Louisiana; you know, Louisiana French. I'm a coonass."

"A what?"

"A Cajun; that's what I am, what we all are down there; a coonie. You know, Coonass . . . . You Catholic?"

"Catholic? No . . . why?"

"I am; all of us are . . . Here comes that sergeant."

"His name's Hatalski—he's okay."

"Rafe, we've got a few minutes yet."

"This is one of the stragglers, Frank; his name's Pardue."

"Rusty Pardue, Sarge."

"You from the Two Nineteenth?"

"Charlie Battery, Sarge."

"What'd you do there?"

"Oh, I spotted some . . . and loaded; fired too. You know, a little of this . . ."

"You've met Rafe here? . . . Good; you stay with him. You hungry?"

"No, Sarge; thanks . . ."

"Can you operate a phone?"

"Sure."

"You'll do that for a while, then. See you, Rafe. . . ."

"He's okay, eh, Ralph?"

"Yeah . . ."

"What's his name again?"

"Hatalski. Frank Hatalski."

"Polish, right?"

"I think so . . ."

"Sure he is; look, all those guys with *ski* are Polish; I knew

14

a whole bunch of them in basic. . . . Where'd you do yours? . . . Your basic?"

"Fort Sill . . . Oklahoma."

"Oh, I know where it is. . . . I've been there too. . . . You like it?"

"Sill? Yeah, it was okay. . . . Are you all right?"

"What do you mean?"

"I mean, are you okay?"

"I'm all right . . . it's just that . . . well, I don't know anybody here. . . ."

"Yeah . . . how about a cigarette?"

"Hey . . . thanks . . . Can I have two more? . . . What'd you do at home? You work?"

"Well, I went to high school and to college, for a year, but my brothers and I, we got some land."

"Ranching, huh? You got a ranch in Texas? With horses and all that?"

"Some, but we mostly do farmwork."

"Yeah? What?"

"Just about everything: cabbage, tomato, carrots, broccoli . . . and cotton."

"Who picks your cotton?"

"What's that?"

"Your cotton; who picks that?"

"Oh . . . We do, and we hire some, too."

"You hire niggers for that?"

"Niggers? Colored?"

"Yeah, you know, black folks for picking . . . That's who picks at home . . . 'Course we pick it, too, but they hire out a lot . . ."

"There aren't that many Negroes in the Valley."

"So who picks it besides you all . . ."

"We do. . . ."

"You're Spanish, right?"

"No; I'm Mexican."

"But you're from Texas?"

"Right."

"Oh . . . When do you all pick? Cotton?"

"Usually from around June to August . . . up to September, just about."

"We don't start till later; we pick in July and then we plow under in late September, early October. . . . You notice the dirt around here?"

"Yeah, it looks pretty bad. . . . It's a hilly place, Korea."

"You can say that again; and rocky, too. . . . You guys dry farm in that place?"

"No . . . we irrigate; we use the river."

"The Rio Grande? Hey, I bet you've been over to Mexico a lot."

"Sure, it's right across."

"Across what?"

"The river; the Rio Grande . . ."

"Oh yeah . . . you got relatives there?"

"Yeah, like I said, it's right across the river . . ."

"And . . . and, you speak Spanish?"

"Sure . . ."

"No shit?"

(Laughs) "Yeah . . ."

"What's so funny?"

"I speak Spanish all the time when I'm home . . ."

"And we speak French, d'ja know that? Yeah. At home. On the street. In the beer joints . . . anywhere . . . Lemme hear you say something in Spanish. . . . Come on, Ralph."

"Rafe . . . ¿Qué quieres que te diga?"

"What'd you just say?"

"I said, 'What do you want me to say?' "

"Hey, d'ja really say that? That's pretty good. Say it again. Come on . . ."

"¿Qué quieres que te diga?"

"Tell you what, you teach . . . hey, here comes Hotski . . ."

"Hatalski . . ."

"Yeah . . ."

3

"The hospital? But that's absurd, Ibby. She's pregnant, that's all. She has the baby, and that's the end of it."

"It isn't that simple, Anna Faye. Graciela says the girl's not strong enough."

"It's even simpler than that, Ibby: she has her baby and then she goes right back to Nicaragua."

"Guatemala."

"One of the two . . ."

"Well, it *is* Guatemala, and the girl needs to be looked to in town. And she's thirteen. . . . And it is Sanford's baby."

"Stop that."

"It is."

"You don't even know that! None of us do."

"He does."

"What's there to be excited about, anyway?"

"I'm not excited, I'm calm, but I won't be calm for too goddam long. Listen to me, Anna Faye: I'm the one that's got to see this thing through. Again."

"Well . . . I . . . I . . . I do too, you know."

"What you want is to ship her out."

"Don't you?"

"But not right now. There may be complications."

"You keep *saying* that."

"Because it's true; because she's very pregnant, and because she's under fucking age."

"Ibb-by! Please!"

"Well, she is, goddammit!"

"All right, what do we do?"

"We fix it, but this is the last goddam time! She's a . . . a . . . a kid, for Christ's sake!"

"Ibby!"

"Listen, sister dear, goddammit: Sanford Blanchard has got *another* maid pregnant. Is that ten, now? Twenty?"

"We'll take care of her . . ."

"This one needs a hospital; we have to take her in to see

Charlie Dean. He may be a piece of absolutely worthless shit, but at least he's a doctor. . . . And he's *ours*."

"Don't be crude, Ibby."

"I'll crude you, Anna Faye. Face it, goddammit: the girl's *preñada;* fat; *panzona;* knocked up; that fucking way; in trouble; *está pa' parir;* the *works*."

"You're terrible."

"Poor damn thing is ugly, ignorant, and illegal. And *we* got her *that way*. In another five months, we chuck her out, fly her out of here, and then twenty a month will feed her and the kid forever . . ."

"Ibby. You make it sound . . ."

"As if Sandy did something bad, Anna Faye? Is that it? That we're sons-of-bitches, Anna Faye? Well, you're goddam right. *He* did and *we* are."

"But what you're saying . . ."

"What I'm saying is that Charlie Dean will tend to her and then operate on Sandy. You hear me? A vasectomy, Anna Faye; it should've been done years ago."

"A *what?* But that . . . why, that's terrible."

"Terrible? We're not talking about some young slick in town here. We're talking about the KLAIL-BLANCHARD-COOKE-RANCH! Anna Faye: he's fifty-six years old, goddammit! He's *my* age! Look: we should've done it years ago."

"You've already said that."

"Yes, goddammit, I've already said that! You keeping count? Well, that old sonofabitch is populating half of Central Goddam America by himself. You keeping count of that too?"

"Oh, Ibby . . ."

"Where is he now?"

"Ah . . ."

"Well?"

"Out."

"Anna Faye, Anna Faye . . . *where* out?"

"To town . . . with Sidney."

"With Sidney? Marvelous! Simply goddam marvelous! Now there's a couple of goddam openers for you . . . just a minute . . . hold it . . . who's driving?"

"Evaristo. . . . He drove them in early this morning."

"Evaristo! Evaristo Garcés is a blind man, Anna Faye. . . . What are those idiots up to now?"

"I think they were going . . ."

"Say it."

"To Mexican town."

"Are. You. Sure?"

"No.... I'm not.... Please, Ibby ... I ... I ... just thought ..."

"What? Just what did you think, goddammit? No . . . you listen. No one's coming into this Ranch with some goddam curandera and her rusty coat hangers, you hear?"

"IBBY!"

"Batshit!"

"Ibby, Evaristo's with them . . ."

"With them? Don't you understand, Anna Faye? The man. Is legally. Blind. Oh, the hell with it. . . . Come on, let's go see the girl."

"She's in the kitchen."

"She's not working, is she?"

"No! She just sits there, that's all."

"We'll bring Graciela with us."

"To Charlie Dean's office?"

"To calm her down. . . . Charlie's to meet us at the clinic first. What *is* her name?"

"Nicéfora."

"Some goddam Guatemalan saint, I'll bet. . . . God, when I think of Sanford . . ."

"Sanford needs help, Ibby."

"Help? You know what he needs? He needs for us to tie a rubber band around his balls so they'll fall off in a week or two."

"Ibby!"

"Shut up, Anna Faye. The last thing I need is for you to try shit an old turd like me."

"Do you *enjoy* talking dirty?"

"Do you *enjoy* cleaning up after Sandy? And where is he *now?* Out with *Sid*ney! And, and, and with Evaristo, for God's sake. . . . Well, shit, at least there's no danger of any of them coming up pregnant, is there?"

"Really, E. B."

"Ree-ah-lly, shit, Anna Faye! You've known about this crap for over twenty years. . . . And what the hell have *you* ever done about it? Zero! *Really, Ibby!* Bullshit, little sister. . . . You've always left it up to Freddie and me to clean up after you and good old *San*ford *Thur*low *Blan*chard himself. Well, no more, Anna Faye. He's a shit, a leech, and a coward. A stinking parasite who's never done one goddam thing for the Family. . . . Son-of-a-bitch has *never* pulled his own weight! But *this* tears it, goddammit! Twenty years of this shit, Anna Faye! Twenty goddam years. . . . Vasectomy, hell!"

"Ibby! Ibb! Please, Ibby . . . you're shaking . . ."

"Vasectomy, hell, Anna Faye! You *hear* me? I'm gonna go cut his goddam pecker off. Is *that* funny?"

"Ibby! You're shaking. . . . Sit down, Ibby. Please, please, Ibby."

"Where the hell are you going?"

"To the kitchen; sit down, Ibby. Please . . . I'm going to get you a glass of water. . . . Where do you keep those pills?"

"I don't *need* those pills; I need that son-of-a-bitch out of here!"

"She'll be gone in a few months, Ibby."

"*She?* Anna Faye, you're not even *close! Him!* Sanford, for Christ's sake. Jesus, Anna Faye!"

"Sit down, Ibby. Please sit down. Please . . . I'll be right back . . ."

Evaristo Garcés, the driver, is a Bank-Ranch Mexican. When he retires (and this will be as soon as Viterbo Longoria dies), Evaristo and Nacha, his wife, will then move from the Ranch to Klail City and on into Viterbo's place. The KBC has always provided for its loyal sons.

Today, though, Evaristo has just run over a dog belonging to a youngster in El Pueblo Mexicano in South Klail, and he's gone over to the youngster's home to explain about the accident.

It's an unpleasant chore, but one that needs to be done. From here, Evaristo will drop off Sanford Blanchard and Sidney Boynton at Chabela Godoy's house.

And (as soon as he settles down) E. B. "Ibby" Cooke will drive Nicéfora Cruz and Graciela Mata to the offices of Charles M. Dean, M.D.

4

"Jehú, Polín Tapia's coming in sometime this afternoon; around three o'clock, I expect. Want to sit in?"

"What's it about?"

"Politics . . . mostly."

"Anything else?"

"Oh, I imagine we'll talk about the Leguizamóns, too . . . it'll be next year's politics, mostly."

"You want me to, Noddy? If you do, I'll stick around."

"You don't like Tapia, do you, Jehú?"

"I think he's a shit . . . but he's got his good side . . ."

"Well, now! How is that?"

"He and P. Galindo are friends . . . and I like P."

"I know you do. . . . What I'm leading up to, Jehú, is: I don't want to have to ask you to stay."

"But you want me to."

"That's right."

"Okay, I'll just tell Esther to........I see; no need to, right?"

"Take a seat, Jehú, there's a few things I want to pass on to you. You want some coffee? Let me call Esther."

Esther Bewley, young and lank, blue-eyed, stringy blond hair. No need for dye or help on *that* hair. Esther is not a secretary, nor a teller, and, definitely, not a clerk. Needed something done? Call Esther. In a hurry? Esther. This, that, and the other? Who else? Pale. Good old English stock with its blood tried, true, and tired. . . . She was *Esther.* You know: *Esther.* Esther Lucille Bewley.

"Esther, when Polín comes in, just lead him in here; if the front door's locked, by then, let him in. He may be a bit late. You got time to dish us some coffee?"

Esther turns to Jehú, smiling. Jehú smiles back; nods; and then winks as he opens the door for Esther Lucille.

"Black, Jehú?"

"Black."

"What was *that* all about?"

"Esther knows about Polín."

"About Polín and you, you mean."

"I'll behave; I always do."

"Ha!.............Hey, did you finally stop smoking? How'd you go about that?"

Polín Tapia is crossing Klail Avenue; first he waited for the light and *then* he looked both ways. Polín wears a hat: Panama for nine months of the year and a felt Stetson for three. It's Panama time in Belken; he's just put his sunglasses away in the case and pats his shirt pocket to check/satisfy/verify their safety. A tug at the belt, a quick check at the pant fly. Damn! When did that shoe get scuffed like that? Damn! Handkerchief out; dab with the tongue. There! Not bad. . . . Right hand raised. Smile. It's señora Salazar: "Pero muy buenos días, señora Salazar." Smile remains. If Arturo Leyva, that idiot son-in-law of señora Salazar wasn't around, I'd show Yolanda Salazar a thing or two . . . (A pipe dream. Arturo Leyva is very much alive and not given to talk.) Polín has forgotten señora Salazar, Arturo, and Yolanda . . . there's the Bank. El First National. . . . Why does Noddy Perkins keep—and that's the only word: keep—why does Noddy keep that, that Malacara person . . . he can't be *that* smart. P. Galindo says he's sharp; but P.'s been wrong before. . . . Shoot! Twelve years ago he said Dewey'd win. . . . Hmph! Shoe doesn't look half bad; must have been back at the curb; or the rail at the Blue Bar. Most likely the rail at the Blue. Jehú Malacara; ha! He's a lost cause. Who *was* that honky tonk special I saw him with? The man's a banker, for Christ's sake! Wonder what Noddy wants? I'd sure like to hook on with the KBC on a permanent basis . . . and maybe the Bank, for starters, anyway. "Where do you work, Mr. Tapia?" "I'm employed at the Bank; I, ah, I work at the First . . . I work with Noddy; ah, Noddy Perkins, don't you know." "Are you still with the Bank, Mr. Tapia?" "Sure am, been there for years." Well, no; not for years—let's see: "Sure am, been there for some time, you know. Been there so long, I might-near forgot *how* long." Yeah, that's better. . . . Oh shit! I've done passed the damned Bank. Was that the Bewley girl I waved to? Why she give me a funny look? Was I moving my lips? Got to watch that. . . . First thing you know, people'll think you're crazy; worse, they'll think you're silly. . . . What's that? Me! My reflection; glass case in pocket; tie straight; belt . . . shoe . . . there she is again; opening the door. Must've been expecting me.

"Good afternoon, young lady."

"Mr. Perkins's waiting for you; Mr. Malacara's in there with him."

What the hell's *he* doing there? "Thank you."

"Here; this way." Noddy didn't say anything about Jehú. . . . "Thank you. . . . Thank you. . . ."

And Esther opens the door.

"Come on in, Polín; make yourself to home. . . . Say hello to Jehú there."

"Polín."

Damn! The kid beat me to it: *I* should've said hello *first*. "Hello, Jehú. Good to see you again." Again? Did I say *again?* What's Noddy going to think?

"Polín . . . sit down. Relax. Whatever it is you're thinking, *stop it*. Relax, now. Come on; settle down. Smoke? Coffee? That's it, settle down. Jehú's here 'cause I told him to. Didn't I, Jehú? See? We're all friends here, Polín, and we need your help. We need your advice on a couple of things. Go on, light up; there's plenty of cups, take one."

It *can't* be politics; I mean, Jehú's here, and what does *he* know? But with Noddy, it's *always* politics. Am I fidgetting? No. "Thank you, Mr. Perkins; this is fine."

"Need some help, Polín; you need to fill in some gaps for us. . . . It's politics, by the way . . ."

A sigh of relief. Polín feels better; secure.

"What can I do for you?"

"What can you tell us about Ira Escobar. Over at the S. L. . . ."

Us? Jehú, too?

"Wake up, Polín. . . . Come on: Jehú's in on this . . . for now."

"Yessir."

"I'm waiting, Polín."

"Well, sir, Ira's a Leguizamón on his mother's side; his father's an Escobar from Barrones, Tamaulipas . . . but *you* know that."

"But Jehú here doesn't. And *I* don't know everything: you do. You all want some *pan de dulce?* Esther can go over to La Nacional for some; biscuits okay? Or do you all prefer *molletes* and that type of thing?"

Merienda. How long is this going to take? Well, hell, might as well dig in. . . . "Yessir, I'll take some of that sweet stuff, you know, *molletes, polvorones*. Anything."

"Esther? Hon . . . go on over to Conrado's place. Bring us a bag of *surtido*. We'll need a fresh pot when you get back. Is that the phone? Who's that, Esther?"

" . . . ."

"No . . . I'm not seeing anybody else today. . . . Right. . . . Thank you, hon. . . . Okay, Polín . . . let 'er rip . . ."

"Ira's married to a Jonesville girl: Rebecca Caldwell; you-all know Catarino Caldwell. I won't go into *that;* her mother's a Navarrete. The Navarretes have relatives on both sides of the River. Some poor, some not. *They're* poor. Not now, of course. Becky, that's Rebecca, got married to Ira, and that helped. They've got two little kids, now. She went to Denton. North Texas?"

"Go on."

"She's nice. Pretty, too. . . . Her mother—when she was young—was a good friend of Viola Barragán . . ."

"You sure about that?"

"Yessir. Want me to go on?"

"Nothing's stopping you, Polín."

What the hell's Jehú here for?

"Polín? Go on."

"Sorry, sir; yessir. They were close; the mother and Viola. . . . Her name's Elvira, Mr. Perkins: Elvira Navarrete. She . . ."

"Yes?"

"She, ah, she's still . . ."

"Looks good?"

"Yes*sir.* She *made* the wedding. She and Ira's mother don't get along."

"And Becky?"

"Well, I hear Becky and her mother-in-law don't get along either."

"And Ira?"

"Ira does what Becky says."

"Is that a fact?"

"Yessir."

"What do *you* think of Ira, Polín?"

"I like him." Damn! I shouldn't have said . . .

"Yeah?"

"He works at the S. and L. Well, you know . . . he . . ." He treats *me* good . . . not like this damn Jehú here. I   hate   that smile. What's so funny, scarecrow?

"Go on."

"Ira's got a degree from St. Mary's. Went to A and M first, though. Don Javier likes him. A lot. The old folks say Ira looks like don Javier did some forty years ago. . . . I don't know how tough Ira is, though." Damn! I . . .

"Go on."

"And . . . ah . . . his Spanish is weak."

24

"How weak is that?"

"Weak-weak."

"Okay. Will he *work* with us?"

"I think so. . . . I *know* so. . . . Yessir, he'll work." I'll *make* him work, that little shit's my ticket to this goddam Bank!

"And I suppose you can work with him? Closely?"

Watch him, does he mean? Sure!

"Yessir; I can work with him."

"Now then, what else can you tell us about our future Commissioner, Place Four?"

Future? Shit! Oh, shit . . . Polín! This.   Is.   It.   You're goddam right I can work with him, you sneaky old son . . .

"Well, Polín . . . what else do I need to know?"

Does that mean that Jehú? Jehú? A Vice P-p-p? Oh, no . . .

"Sir?"

"What else is there, Polín? About Ira?"

"Nothing bad, sir . . . he likes politics."

"Does he now?"

"He's pretty smooth, sir." If they bring Ira *here* . . . does that mean that Jehú is *out?* Or . . . a V. P.? God, no; not a V. P. . . . No, please. Please.

"Sounds good; you'll be a big help in next year's elections, Polín. . . . By the way, Johnnie Hufsteder says he may need someone at Klail Paint."

I want to work for the KBC. The KBC, Noddy.

"What do you say, Polín?"

It's a start, I guess . . .

"Sounds good, sir. I've got experience in that, you know."

"I know that. . . . It's a *start,* Polín . . ."

"Yessir."

"Now . . . we're going to run against Roger Terry; find out what he's been up to lately. You need about a month or so for that?"

"Yessir, I'll get on it."

"We're opening an election account next week, and you can start drawing on it beginning then; we'll talk more about the KBC Paint Store later on, too."

Hot-hot-hot damn! Hot Damn! Why doesn't the man keep a mirror in this office? Goddammit . . . am I smiling? I   don't want   to   give   myself   away. Steady now. Watch the voice:

"Well, sir. (Good, Polín) (cough cough) I'll do my best. (Good! No shaking now. . . . Mind the shakes. . . .) Yessir . . . I'll do my best."

"I know you will. Esther? You in there? She's not back yet."

"Hungry? Who's hungry? I'm in! In!"

"You okay, Polín?"

"Oh, yessir . . . if you all will excuse me, I'll skip the coffee and cookies and stuff."

"You don't have to start on Roger Terry this very minute, Polín. . . . You sure you won't stay for a fresh pot?"

I want to get the hell *away* from *here!* IwanttogototheBlueBar. I want to tell the guys there: "I'm working for the Ranch, goddammit!"

"Okay, Polín, have it your own way. . . . Now, remember, not a word. To anyone."

Nothing? To anyone? PLEASE.

"Not a word, Polín; just tell 'em you're on retainer here; you're doing some special collecting for the Bank."

"Yessir."   The Bank!   "Yessir."

"On your way, now. Call me anytime, now."

"Yessir."

Outside, the sun was, well, not exactly shining. It was beaming and smiling upon Antonio Apolinar Tapia, the son of Domingo Tapia. Beaming? Radiating, goddammit! Polín! Polín! You're in the Bank! The Bank! What are those fools looking at? Just who do they think they are? Just who the hell do they think *I* am? I'm Polín Tapia, goddammit. . . . That's who, and I work for Noddy Perkins. You *got* that? Wait'll P. Galindo hears *this*. . . . Shit: I'll buy the first round. First? Second and third, goddammit. This is the *big* time, and it feels *good*.

5

"Well, Noddy, did he actually *demand* we take on this nephew of his?"

"Oh, no; old Javier doesn't operate that way. You know that; I'm sorry, Ibby, you were going to say . . ."

"Noddy's on target, Junior. I've known and dealt with Javier Leguizamón 20-30 years now, and . . . well, he won't demand, but he'll hint around enough. *Do* we have anything for him?"

"Any ideas, Noddy?"

"One."

"Let's hear it, then. Ibby?"

"Nothing, let's hear what Noddy has to say."

"About a year ago, make that a year and a half ago, I told Jehú he didn't have what it took to be a County Commissioner."

"Just like that?"

"Well, words to that effect. . . . Anyway, Jehú doesn't care for the job, besides that, he's got enough to do here."

"No complaints, Noddy. What do you have, then?"

"First of all, who's the nephew? What's his name?"

"Ira. Ira Escobar."

"Escobar? From Klail? Which Escobar's that?"

"No, they're from Jonesville; right, Junior?"

"Yes; the boy's mother is a Leguizamón, Noddy. That's where it comes from."

"He can't be too swift around the track, I don't imagine."

"Probably not. . . . *Have* you come up with something?"

"I may, and it may take some time to talk it through. Both of you free right now?"

"I am; Ibby?"

"No. Ben and I are going to Edgerton this afternoon."

"If it's the gas plant business, that can wait."

"I'll have to call Ben then."

"You do that. . . . Wait a minute, Ibby; you know, it may be better if Ben sits in on this after we're through. Don't call Ben; have Esther do it."

"Esther?"

"Yessir?"

"Call Mr. Timmens and tell him we're not going to Edgerton, but for him to come here instead. Now."

"Yessir."

"Now then, let's hear what Noddy has to say."

"First of all, it's not a spur of the moment thing, and second, when I sketch this out, you'll see Ben's part in it."

"Let's hear it, Noddy."

"Jehú's not going to work out for county politics . . ."

". . . or any other."

". . . and he's doing a good job here. I haven't heard anything about his personal life that could hurt us or him."

"Is Esther still on this?"

"Ibby, let's just say that Jehú trusts her."

"Go on, Noddy."

"So . . . that's settled, right? On the Leguizamón problem . . ."

"Concern, Noddy."

"Problem-Concern . . . on the Leguizamón *thing,* then, we can do it in such a way that we can have what we want."

"Which is?"

"Well, that's where Ben comes in."

"Get to it, Nod."

"Here it is: we take that Escobar boy into the S. and L."

"Javier wants the boy at the Bank."

". . . we take him into the S. and L., a year, a year and a half, and *then* the First."

"But . . ."

"Listen: after a year or whatever, we talk to him about the Commissioner's race."

"But will he want it? You were wrong on Jehú, you know."

"Only on the politics side, Ibby. . . . Ready? We put Ira Escobar against Roger Terry."

"Ha! A Mex against an Anglo? In 1960? In Belken?"

"*Our* Mex, Ibby."

"Go on, Noddy."

"We buck young Terry. . . . Hard."

"And how hard is that?"

"Hard-hard, Junior."

"Money?"

"Money."

"I'm sure you've got something else; you always do."

"That's the tip of the ice-verga, as they say. . . . Here's some more: Ira'll beat Roger in the primaries, and Roger'll run as an independent in the generals in November."

"Hold on, Nod; that's a mighty long shot."

"Go on, Noddy."

"You're going to like this: Roger'll run in the generals; he'll get some Mex support. I know what he's got. . . . Now: Roger will run. We'll harass here and there, and then we pull the plug on Hap Bayliss."

"*What?*"

"Yeah, Noddy. Run that one by again, will you?"

"Hap Bayliss?"

"Keep it down, Ibby. . . . Nod: you were saying?"

"Ira'll run like a son-of-a-bitch; I'll see to that; Javier'll see to that. We get Polín Tapia and some of the Mex po-li-ti-cos on this. . . . Now, after Roger loses the primary . . ."

"Noddy!"

"Let him finish, Ibby."

"Roger runs in the general, and that's okay. We step on some toes, call in some debts and . . . favors . . . you know. This'll take some time, of course. Hap announces his intentions to continue to serve the people of Belken County as he has in the past, etcetera, etcetera. . . . About a month before the November generals, a month or so, I haven't thought this out. . . . Eeny-way, around that time, Hap announces he's ill; sick. A very sick man."

"Shit!"

"Ibby, please. Go on, Nod."

"Hap announces that he wants all of his friends . . ."

"Ha!"

". . . to vote for his young, talented, and long time friend: Roger Terry."

"What was that?"

"Roger will be in the fold by then."

"And *how* do you propose to do just that?"

"Keep it down, Ibby . . . go on, Noddy."

"Ira gets Place Four, Roger goes to Washington . . ."

"And Hap?"

". . . and Hap gets retired."

"Where does Ben fit into this puzzle of yours?"

"All in good time, Ibby. Now, we all know about Hap's problem, and we've done a good job on that . . . but something's come up."

"Is it bad, Noddy? Family?"

"Bad enough. Sammie Jo found one of those love lockets . . ."

"And what the hell are those?"

"I don't know what you call 'em. It's a goddam trinket; heart shaped, you know. You put pictures in 'em and wear 'em around the neck."

"Go on, Noddy."

"Sammie Jo ran across it by the pool: damn thing belongs to Hap or to Sid . . ."

"Well, shit . . ."

"Ib . . ."

"It's getting out of hand . . ."

"Noddy. Noddy, we should've been told of this before now . . ."

"I just found out last night. Late . . . Sammie Jo came in at four; woke me up. Well, when the Leguizamón thing came up, I figured we could put everything together . . ."

"I'm sorry, Noddy."

"If you're thinking about Sammie Jo, Junior, don't worry about it. She's certainly known about her own husband, but it was Hap, see . . ."

"I understand."

". . . godfather and all. And now this."

"Well, ah . . . is Ben going to talk to Hap, then?"

"Ben talks to Edith; *I* talk to Hap. But not just now."

"Now then, all this aside, what about the rest of it?"

"It'll take some doing, Junior, but it isn't impossible, I mean, hell . . . it might even get interesting for a while."

"And Ben, Noddy?"

"Yes, Noddy; he and Hap are brothers-in-law, goddamit!"

"Well, first of all, I'm not thinking of sending Ben back to D.C. What we need him for is to talk to Edith like I said . . . and then . . ."

"And then?"

"And then to pass the word on to some of our folks."

"Let me ask you this: is the Bowly Ponder loan tied to this? In any way?"

"I did that as a future, but we may need him for this one. I want us to be ready."

"Good enough. And is that it for Ben?"

"No . . . I think we need some advice from that end of it, too. We have all the financial information we need, of course, but Roger Terry's an attorney, and Ben may fill in some gaps for us; clients, deals, you know."

"What do you think Edith'll say to all this?"

"She doesn't have to know everything. . . . Holy, holy . . . it's times like these when I think about Freddie . . . she'd be in her glory, wouldn't she?"

30

"I'll say. . . . Well, what about Jehú?"

"Let's not get into that yet. . . . You called it a puzzle, Ibby, and I'd like to go over some of the pieces. . . . Nod?"

"Sounds chancy to you, does it?"

"No; not at all. But why don't we just go step by step; a check-list."

"Right. Jehú's out—never really was in. Ira Escobar is a Leguizamón, and Junior is sure that he'll run—if we ask. That's set."

"Ibby?"

"No questions."

"Go on, Noddy."

"It begins with Hap, and we'll work down to Roger which then brings us to Ira again. There's some side stuff, and it'll come up as we go along."

"Hap's problem is partly ours, mostly his. Sid's the side issue here, and I hate to do this, but Sammie Jo is going to have to live with *this* mistake."

"Good."

"Roger . . . Roger's a liberal, but it stops with the pocketbook. Side issue? His wife . . . and she can help us: Bowly Ponder can stop her for speeding and reckless driving now and then; maybe even a citation. Harold Fikes can help there."

"I think Noddy's on the right track; I'd like to mention something about the voting . . . no, I'm not going into a breakdown . . . but, Belken's going to know, needs to know, we're against Roger. And another *but* is that the U.S. Rep's job is a Valley-wide affair . . ."

"And?"

"The tricky part is to beat Roger without him looking like a complete son-of-a-bitch; you know, he'll lose the Commissioner's post, but he's got to look acceptable for November. . . . I know we can work it out, it's just a reminder."

"No, it's a good point."

"What's the matter, Junior?"

"It's Hap—everything sounds convincing enough, and I know we're on the right track and all that, but . . . what do we do with Hap?"

"Well, we can put some Ranch hand . . . to drive him around; watch him; keep an eye on him."

"But for how long, Ibby? Look, Hap's been talking about retiring for four years now . . . we've pushed and shoved to keep him up there, and he won't be *that* disappointed when we tell him of our plans for Roger in November. Hap may even be relieved to hear the news. . . . Ben handles that end, we're agreed, but, what do we do with Hap after the elections?"

"Yes, his, uh, preferences could embarrass us . . ."

"Yes . . . I'm afraid that it'll take more thought than I'm prepared to give it right now, so why don't we do what we each have to do, and worry about Hap after November. Noddy? Ibby?"

"Fine."

"Okay."

"Now, what about Jehú?"

"He may help; he's a good speaker; a preacher almost."

"I was thinking about the Leguizamóns and . . ."

"Oh, *that,* yeah, well, if Jehú doesn't help, may not want to in fact, he won't hinder. I know him. Now, I don't know if he knows Ira . . ."

"Ira married?"

"Yep; she's a Caldwell."

"Anglo?"

"No . . . her father's a half Mex and half soldier . . . out of Fort Jones."

"Who's her mother? Is that the Leguizamón connection?"

"No, remember? Ira's *mother* is the Leguizamón; I don't know the girl's mother. But I *can* tell you who'd know. For a fact."

"Who's that?"

"Tell him, Junior."

"Viola."

"Say no more. . . . Here: I'll fill Ben in on this. You going to call Javier, Noddy?"

"Well, I think it would look better if *I* called Javier."

"I think so, too, Junior. Hell, I *know* so . . ."

"It's settled, then; we bring in that boy to the S. and L., and then on to the First later on, and when Cutchie McLemore retires, we get two Mexicans on the County Court, and we get Hap out and Roger in. . . . It's going to be interesting, boys . . ."

"Ha! You sound like old Rufus Three."

"And that's a compliment, Junior."

6

"Time to call in, Rusty. Rusty! Call-in time . . ."

"Oh . . . okay . . . Badger Four. Over. Badger Three calling in."

"What's up?"

"Everything's okay up here. . . . Over."

"Understood. Out."

". . . Well, that's that. . . . How long now?"

"One more hour, and that's it."

"Hey . . . how far are we from home?"

"What?"

"Home. How far are we from *home*? You know, miles. How many miles are we from home?"

"I don't know . . . five . . . six thousand?"

"Nah; it's got to be more than that."

"Okay."

"No—come on; how far are we, Rafe?"

(Laugh) "I don't know. . . . It's a long way, that's all."

"I bet it's . . . I bet it's nine thousand miles."

"I guess so . . ."

"Don't you think about home? Don't you have anything back there?"

"I think about home all the time . . ."

"I do too. . . . What do you think about?"

"I think about home, that's all. Home. People. I think about home, that's all."

"I do too; I think about it all the time. . . . I think about it, well, I think about it, you know. I think about home. You?"

"So do I, Rusty."

"I wonder how far it is?"

(Laugh) "I don't know; it's a long way."

"How far is it from where you live . . . to, ah, the state of Washington? Fifteen hundred?"

"Fifteen hundred, two thousand miles . . . I really don't know, Rusty."

"Okay, say two thousand, and how far is it to Hawaii? No; we didn't go to Hawaii. . . . Right? Okay . . . let's see: how far it is then from Washington to Japan? Four, five thousand miles, right? What do you think?"

"Sounds right."

"Well, I'll bet it's no less than five thousand miles and you're two thousand miles, right? And, well, we're not too far from Japan from here, but, how far would you say we are from where my Dad lives in Elton? How far are you from Elton, Louisiana?"

"I don't know. Five? Six hundred miles?"

"How far are you from Houston again?"

"About four hundred."

"Yeah, six sounds about right . . . 'cause we're pretty close to two hundred miles. From Houston. Sooooo, I figure, ah, I figure from Elton to Washington, ah, it's about twenty five hundred miles and then another five. . . . We're about seven thousand five hundred miles from home."

"Yeah, I guess we are . . ."

"You think about it, ha?"

"Yeah . . . I think about it all the time."

"Me too. I got a lot of friends back home. You?"

"Yeah . . . I've got some (laughs) friends. Everybody's got some friends."

"Yeah? Well, I've got a *lot* of friends. I have . . . I've got a *lot* of friends at home. A *lot*."

7

Are we to believe that Noddy Perkins' best laid plans will work out? To perfection? There are, of course, certain imponderables; to name but one: the Leguizamóns. They may just not want for Ira Escobar to serve an apprenticeship at the Klail City Savings and Loan; that is, Javier Leguizamón (and his niece, Vidala—Ira's mother) may want for Ira to go straight to the bank. Sample comment: "Really, now, if that, that, what's his name? . . . that, that Malacara person is at the Bank, why, Ira surely *should* be!"

Javier, again, of course, doesn't work that way; never has. As for pressure from his niece, love or some other feeling, perhaps, would move him: not pressure. And, certainly, not from her. And, besides, she misses the point of it all: Javier wants Ira in for the looks of it; it looks *good,* as it were; for the Leguizamóns. The Commissioner's consideration—when Javier learns of it—will be the clincher.

At this point, almost anything could go wrong (of course, of course) but Noddy, who had married into the KBC, would try and do his damndest that nothing went wrong. A by the way: nothing went wrong.

One failing of Noddy's is that compulsive "I'd rather do this myself" drive of his; on the asset side, neither Ibby nor Junior Klail would mix with the Mexicans. That much, anyway . . . Noddy would. For business reasons. But he would, and so, the KBC, unable to fail or to flounder, was steered, locally, by Noddy.

E. B. "Ibby" Cooke had other fish to fry: he was Family and so was Junior. Noddy, brother-in-law and all, was not Family. His daughter, Sammie Jo was; but not Mr. Arnold Perkins himself. Be it understood: Ibby didn't see Noddy as a hired hand. Fair is fair: Ibby didn't dwell on Noddy, and, if he ever did happen to think on his brother-in-law . . . but why am I saying all this since you know Ibby's theme: Noddy's not family; he's necessary; he's a hard worker; he sees things through; etc. But it was that everlasting BUT HE'S NOT F.

Yes.

As for Junior Klail: he *ran* the Bank; Noddy made the moves;

in fact, Noddy did everything but run the Bank. Now, the tellers, the commercial lenders, the secretaries, the clerks, the typists, the, the, the janitors, for God's sake, *knew* that Noddy ran the Bank. Noddy, of course, knew better, as did Junior Klail.

It was only natural that Noddy chafed, but in the end, it was Rufus T. Klail V. Junior to one and all.

Noddy also knew that he hadn't done bad for someone with an eighth grade education. It wasn't enough, either, because Noddy, too, had had his own dreams; but, at sixty-two, he knew where he was: married to the Bank, and, in some ways, still married and, in some ways, still in love with Blanche Cooke: Blanche was sick and given to drink. Some would even call her an alcoholic. And there was Sammie Jo, an only child. Pretty enough; and brainy (it was in the Family). So far unproven and two marriages behind her: 1) Theodore P. Bradshaw, of the Dellis County Bradshaws (and he *was* an alcoholic), and 2) Sidney Boynton (Otis Boynton's) and "as queer as they come." *No Perkins blood to pass along, unless . . . no, no, not that.

So: there wasn't much Noddy *could* do, except make money for the Bank—moving, he called it—and seeing to the KBC's interests and, and . . .

Noddy was convinced (and mistaken as we all know) that without him, the KBC, Klail, Belken County—the whole goddam Valley, as it were—would go straight to hell were it not for him. . . . And, and, yes!, at sixty-two, he too needed warmth, companionship. Understanding. That was it: understanding. Comprehension, even. A woman, goddammit! And so, at sixty-two, but that KBC which wouldn't go away, which (without him) would sink, die and disappear into the chaparral bushland, weighed on Noddy almost as much as his own needs. And so, he would grab the nearest available maid. At the KBC. But Noddy, ever careful Noddy Perkins, always took care. Always.

Did Sammie Jo know . . . suspect? If . . . but she was kind; understanding, too. Yes, if anyone understood, it was Sammie Jo.

And Noddy was not an animal. A brute. He needed . . . a, a, a, an outlet. That was it: an outlet. Sixty-two! Goddammit, sixty-two, "But I still can." And he could; and he did.

But as Ibby said, "He's not Family."

---

*According to Noddy, Ibby, Freddie, et. al.

8

"You got a girl back home, Rafe? I don't mean someone serious, you know; I mean, a girl . . . any girl. You know. Someone to write to. Once in a while?"

"No . . . you?"

"I did; ah, I guess I still do—now and then; she was born there in Elton, and I met her when me and my Dad moved there, but then they moved on out to Eunice; that's a big town. Her father's pretty handy with his hands, and he knows a lot about tools, see? His name's Pros*per*. . . . Her name's Suzy. Suzy Postelle. She's kinda . . . skinny, but she's nice. And quiet . . . and real nice. But you must have had a girl in school, right?"

"I was married once, and . . ."

"Hey, I didn't know that. What happened?"

"It was right after I got out of the Army, and . . ."

"You been in before? I *thought* you had. Why'd you come back for?"

"I went in right after high school; a whole bunch of us did. . . . And we got out about the same time; we all went in for a short time, eighteen months."

"Yeah?"

"Yeah . . . and then I got married, and I went to junior college for a year, and I worked on the farm, but we planned for me to go to school . . . to college."

"College? Hey!"

"Yeah . . . but she died, Rusty."

"Died? She *died?* No......."

"She drowned . . ."

"Oh, Jesus . . . I'm sorry. . . . No; damn! I, I'm sorry, man. Jesus . . ."

"It's okay; I can talk about it . . . now. The reserve called me up right after that; called the other guys, too. Charlie, Joey, Sonny, you know. . . . Called up a cousin of mine, too."

"Who's he? You got a cousin, too?"

"I've got a whole bunch of cousins. . . . This one's special; you'd like him, Rusty; he's . . ."

"Yeah? What's he like?"

"He's a pretty good guy. . . . He's over here some place."

"No shit? Your cousin is? In Japan or out here?"

"Last I heard, he was here, down in Pusan . . . yeah . . . he's a real good guy."

"Hey, I'm sorry about your wife; I mean . . . you know . . ."

"It's okay . . ."

"Gosh, how old are you, then? Twenty-two!"

"Twenty-one in January . . ."

"Coming up? Oh, man, we got to celebrate; no two ways about it. . . . Yeah, no shit, we got to. . . . Tell you what, we'll get some guys out. . . . You know . . . we'll get drunk, right? Like we did in Japan last Christmas? Remember? Over at......at that place . . ."

"The whorehouse?"

"Yeah, *there* . . . that was *good,* wasn't it?"

"Yeah; it was good . . ."

"Hey, man, I'm sorry about . . . you know."

"It's okay, Rusty; I can talk about it . . ."

"My Mom died, too. Yours?"

"Yeah . . ."

"And your Dad?"

"Yeah . . ."

"But you got your two brothers . . . and all those cousins, right?"

"Yeah, sure . . ."

"Boy, that's nice. . . . I only got *one* brother, and he lives in Lufkin, that's in East Texas. . . Angelina County? His wife's from up there . . . and that's where he lives . . . my Dad . . . he, ah, doesn't work anymore. . . . He's disabled, you know what I mean? That's when we moved from Ruston to Elton. . . . But he's a pretty nice old guy. . . . I like him. He's a good man, but he doesn't know how to write, see, and I send him my allowance *every* month, and it's okay. . . . So you got a cousin here?"

"Yeah, and you'd like him; trouble is, I don't have his address . . ."

"Maybe you could write home and get it. . . . Know what I mean? Say, that's silly, isn't it? I mean, you got to write *there* to get his address *here?* It'd be good, wouldn't it . . .? Wouldn't it? And meet him? When you going to write home the next time?"

9

At the KBC. Poolside.

"Jesus Christ, Sidney! Hap *Bayliss!* How could you? My God, Sid, he's an old *man.* Oh . . . why do I even *try?.......*There's just no talking to you, is there?"

"Do *I meddle?*"

"Shit!"

"All right, if that's the way you want it, said the sailor, what Mexican are you fucking *now?*"

"Goddam you!"

"Let's see, is Rafe Buenrostro still available? Or how about that cousin of his that Noddy hired; you know, the one with the funny name?"

"Fuck *you,* Sid."

"My card's filled, thank you."

"You disgusting son-of-a-bitch . . ."

"Temper . . . temper . . . Sammie Jo . . ."

"You low-life bastard!"

"Hardly one or the other, Sammie Jo. . . . Sam! *Look* at me! Come on; hold *still,* will you? Look at me! Okay? Now, we *both* knew exactly what we were getting . . ."

"Oh, hell, don't you start on *that* shit again."

"Well?"

"You *don't* understand, Sid . . . I'm angry because . . . because I *love* you!"

"And I love *you,* Sammie Jo."

"Christ! Don't *say* it that way."

"I take it back; I apologize. . . . Sam? I love *you.* Very much."

"But why *Hap,* Sid?"

"Why not?"

"He's, he's . . . oh, for God's sakes, Sid, he's an *old* man! And, and, wrinkled . . . and dirty . . . and . . ."

"He loves me, Sam, and I *need* him. What else is there?"

"But. You're. Thirty. Years. Old. He . . . he's *fifty* . . . fifty-five; *isn't* he, Sid?"

"That's enough, Sammie Jo. I don't want you to make *any* reference to Hap's age again, hear?"

"I'm sorry, Sid; but . . . Gee-zuz! It's just that . . ."

"Is it Rafe, Sam?"

"No! Goddammit!"

"I'm sorry, Sam; and I'm sorry for whatever it was *I* said. . . . Here, have a drink."

"No!"

"You know, it'd be easier for you if you took a drink now and then. . . . Well, never mind *that.* Want to talk about it? You can talk to *me,* you know, girl to girl."

"Oh, Sid, please . . ."

"You *have* to laugh at it once in a while, Sam. It helps. . . . Smile, Sam! Now: *what* is it or *who* is it this time? . . . It *is* Rafe, isn't it?"

"Yes . . . it's him again . . ."

"Well?"

"I love him, Sidney . . ."

"You can't, Babe; *you're* in love with *me,* remember?"

"Help me, Sid; please . . ."

"Oh, Sam, I'm not . . ."

"Okayokayokay . . ."

"There! Look at you: you're beginning to look better already."

"Here, go on . . . light this for me. . . . Thanks . . . Thanks. . . . Well, anyway . . . Rafe . . . Rafe's a *shit!"*

"I hardly know the boy."

"Be serious, Sid."

"I am."

"Anyway, he and I are *good* together. *Really* good, but he's still a shit."

"And?"

"And? It's im*por*tant that *I* drop *him!* Shit! OH! I don't know *what* to do!"

"I do. Drop him, Sam . . . he'll come back; they always do."

"Oh!"

"Although . . ."

"Yes?"

"It doesn't matter. Listen to this: you've got *me;* you've got friends, relatives, and *time. Time,* Sam. Look, let's take off for a few days you and I. Together. What do you say. You're bored, Sam, and he's not worth it. Is he? *Is* he? Of *course* not. *No* one is. Let me tell you something: what *you* need is a va*ca*tion; you need to get away . . . away from Klail and away from the Valley. . . . Go up to Houston, Sam; forget him. . . . Make *him* sweat."

"He won't. The son-of-a-bitch won't even pick up the phone."

"Houston's the answer, then. Tell you *what:* let's you and I go up to Houston *together.*"

"The *two* of us?"

"Come *on,* let's do it. It'd be good for the both of us. I know of some great new *spots* there . . ."

"It's no good, Sidney . . ."

"Sure it is. . . . I'll be out of the way. What do you say?"

"Oh, Sid . . ."

"Come *on;* call the hangar. We can be there in two-three hours, Sam. Two hours, think of it! Come *on,* Sam. Fun, Sam. Fun! Forget the Mex. . . . Let's have a smile, come on. Come *on* . . . good! Gooooood!"

"Sid . . . do you even think that you and I . . ."

"Babe, we've *been* through that, and you'd just wind up getting hurt again. . . . Look: I'm a *fag,* and I don't *mind!* A-tall. I'm *happy.* . . . Can you under*stand* that? I know what I *am:* I'm a *joke,* and I don't *care. We're* special people you and I. And: I do *love* you, Sam. Very much."

"I know you do . . ."

"See? No more argument. . . . Gone, faded away. . . . Here, give us a kiss. . . . Look, *I'll* call the hangar and *you* call the Graymont. . . . How long do you want to stay?"

"Is a week too much?"

"Let's try it, we've always got *this* to come back to, you know."

"Is it okay?"

"What do you mean, Sam?"

"Tearing off like this . . ."

"Of *course,* it is."

"I don't know . . ."

"Come on, don't back out *now,* Sammie Jo. *Please.* For me."

"Do you love me, Sid?"

"Very much, Sam . . ."

"We'll have fun, won't we, Sid?"

"Of course we will."

"And you think it's okay?"

"Why *shouldn't* we, Sam? *We* have special needs, you and I. We *deserve* this, Sammie. Hang on to that."

"I'll never leave you, Sid. Never."

"And I love you, too, Sam. . . . Go on: call the Graymont, and then pick out something nice for me to wear . . ."

It's an arrangement.

10

"Fog's clearing . . ."

"Yep."

"What time is Rafe supposed to get here?"

"Can't be too long . . . I imagine chow's about over . . ."

"Yeah . . . I was just . . . oh-oh . . . Rusty? Rusty. . . . What's that all about?"

"What are you talking about?"

"Well, I don't know. Looks like . . . Looks like there's about sixty of our guys down there."

"Where?"

"Here: take a look."

"Where?"

"Turn to the right. See Two-Tit Mountain?"

"Yeah."

"Okay: go to the right one. Now, come on down to the belly button. Got it? Now, from the belly button, go to three o'clock. Four. Five . . ."

"Oh, shit."

"You see them?"

"Yeah, there's about seventy of our guys down there . . . chowing down. . . . Hold it . . ."

"What's the matter?"

"Shit, that's no seventy guys: that's more like a hundred and fifty or sixty of 'em down there. What the hell are they doing? Isn't that a firing lane?"

"I don't think so. . . . What the hell *is* that, Rusty? Is that a patrol?"

"If it is, that's the biggest goddam patrol I've ever seen. What the *hell* are they doing down there? Ned, are you sure that's not a firing lane?"

"I'm checking...................No; it's okay."

"When'd you see them?"

"Just now, when the fog burned off and all . . ."

"Hmph . . . well, I'm going to call Brom and let him know just the same."

"Why don't we just wait until Rafe gets here; it'll be just a few more minutes."

"Holy shit!"

"What?"

"*You* look through these now. Look!"

"Where?"

"To the left, by where Brom should be."

". . . Gee-zuz! Those guys are Chinks."

"Damn right. How many, you think?"

"Let's see. . . . Oh, sweet Jesus, there must be two, three hundred of 'em."

"At least, yeah."

"Man, look at what the fog brought in . . ."

"Yeah."

"Ta-hell's going on, though?"

"I don't know . . . let's see, looks like they're between us and Brom."

"You sure?"

"Well, shit, they're about a thousand yards away, and Brom's what? Twelve, thirteen hundred yards . . . a mile, right?"

"Hey, here comes Rafe . . . get down, Rafe."

"What?"

"Down! Get down!"

"What the hell's going on?"

"Take a peek.......Here.......No, no, right down there..........Well?"

"Goddam! That's a lot of people down there."

"Isn't *that* the truth. Now, look to the left. What do you see?"

"Shit! Those guys are Chinks . . ."

"What do you think, Rafe?"

"I don't know . . . they're all chowing down. . . . One thing though: they haven't seen each other."

"Yeah? How do you figure that?"

"Cause there's a couple of rises between them. . . . Ta-hell's going on?"

"That's what we're wondering."

"Well, shit, give me the phone."

"What are you going to do?"

"I'm going to call Bromley up."

"Rafe, you think it's safe?"

"Safe? Goddam, Ned, they went right by him. Let's see if he's alive or holed up or something. . . . Hold it a minute . . ."

"Yeah? What's the matter?"

"You. Are you okay, Ned?"

"Yeah; why?"

"You sure you're okay?"

"Yeah, I'm fine."

"Okay . . . I'm calling Brom right now. Rusty, what's Brom's call?"

"I think he's Badger Three."

"Okay. Get batallion on the line, Rusty; tell 'em to hold on till I get through to Brom. Tell Hat I'm on the other line, and tell him about our guys over by Tit. Okay?"

"Any chance they cut the wire?"

"We'll see.........There, it's ringing. . . . Badger One? I mean, Badger Three . . . Aw, shit: Brom!"

"Hey, Rafe; you okay, buddy?"

"Yeah. . . . You, ah, you see any Chinks out there?"

"What are you talking about?"

"I'm saying: you see any Chinks out there?"

"At this hour of the goddam morning?"

"Behind you, Brom."

"What's wrong with you?"

"Look, Brom, there's some Chink infantry between you and us up here. They're about three hundred yards behind you."

"No shit?"

(Sigh) "Brom . . . what are you doing?"

"Well, I'm looking up front."

"Not up front, goddammit. Turn around and put your glasses on. . . . Now, what do you see?"

"Holy shit! There must be close to a couple-a-hundred guys back there."

"We figure closer to three or four. . . . Listen, now: we've also got close to two hundred of *our* guys to the right. You got that?"

"Yeah? What the hell's going on?"

"I don't know, Brom, but I'm thinking of bringing some mortars in."

"Mortars? Shit; that won't do it."

"You want us to call in some artillery, then? Right on top of you?"

"Hell, yes . . ."

"How deep can you go?"

"Deep enough . . . really, Rafe . . . Rafe?"

"Now, I don't know what our troops are doing out there, but we got to get them out before we fire on the Chinks 'cause once we start up, then the Chink artillery'll open up."

"Yeah?"

"Well, we get ours out of the way on the double . . ."

"Yeah?"

"And when that's clear, we start on the guys down there. . . . Now, Brom: you're going to have to tuck. Deep. Hold it a minute, Brom; hang on. Rust, you got batallion yet? Good. . . . Brom! Brom! Okay: when the shit hits, I figure they'll cut and run down the same way they came up: right at you. They sure as hell can't go to the sides; that's too goddam steep for 'em . . . so, they'll run like hell and right back at you. You're going to have to put up with a lot of shit . . . you know: first ours and then theirs . . ."

"Go ahead."

"Give us a few minutes to get Batallion to get those guys moving."

"Check."

"Don't hang up, Brom; leave the line on, I don't want any ringing."

"Gotcha . . ."

"Rust, you still got Hat on the line?......Good.......Hat? Rafe. Hat, we got some Chinks about a thousand yards up front........No, they're chowing down.........Bromley..............Yeah, but there's a snag: we got some two hundred of our guys over by Two-Tit.......We don't know, but if you can move them, Rust and Ned'll work out the coordinates for this place................Yeah........Okay, hang on, I gotta get back to Brom. Hey, Brom! . . . . Look, it'll be a few more minutes; you hang on for a little while. Ned and Rusty and I are getting the stuff ready for Batallion. Hang on. . . . Okay? Stay on the line now."

"Go ahead."

"How you guys coming?"

"It's all here."

"Okay. Hat? Hat? Rafe............that's good. Good! Listen. Rust'll give you the poop, I gotta get back to Brom. See you . . . Brom!"

"Go ahead."

"Hat says our guys are moving out now. Here goes: we've got every bit of ground sensed, and we're going to shell the shit right out of them. Rusty's passing all the coordinates to Batallion . . . yeah, all of them and in sequence of fire. Got that? Now, we're going to fire past you all the way to Eddie Boy Ridge."

". . . Eddie Boy Ridge; got it."

"After you and I sign off here, you then count for three minutes and after that we'll open up short and then long. We're going to stop two hundred yards short of you and then, two minutes later, we're going to fire two hundred yards further up . . ."

"Two hundred yards . . ."

"We'll wait another two minutes after that. Got it?......Okay. And then, we're going to fire all the way to Eddie Boy at hundred yards intervals: Able, Baker, Charlie; Charlie; Able; Baker; and like that. . . ."

"You'll be spotting hundreds all the way to the Ridge. . . ."

"Good boy! Listen: Ned's got his eyes on the Chinks and Rusty's looking to ours; so don't worry about *our* guys. I'm going to start counting, Brom, and it's going to start raining shit down there. You tuck in now. Wad up. I'm signing off; I've still got Hat on the line and you've got three minutes, Brom, three minutes starting: NOW!

"Hat? We're all set..........We'll be okay..........Sure.....Yeah. . . . Yeah............Okay.......*Right*.....*Okay,* I'll watch him. Over and out and all that good shit, Hat. What? Right; see you, now."

11

"I'm not a nymphomaniac, goddammit. I can take it or leave it. I prefer to take it, but that doesn't make me a nympho; or a goddam lesbian, either. And fuck Sidney Boynton . . . if he only could!

"I'm not; I'm not; I'm not. I'm Sammie Jo Perkins. I'm Sammie Jo Perkins Bradshaw; Sammie Jo Perkins Bradshaw *Boynton* and Rafe Buenrostro's a shit!

"Just who the hell does he think he is? Goddam you, Rafe. . . . You bastard. You Mexican son-of-a-bitch. . . . Who do you think you are, anyway? I'll be goddammed if I *ever* call you again. . . . Go on, lose that goddam eye. Who cares? Lose it, you son-of-a-bitch, and then the Mexicans'll call you Tuerto. Serve you right. Bastard. Who needs you? I can get anybody. And I got myself. Ooooooooh, there!

"Why doesn't he call *me?* All he has to do is to pick up the phone, stick his finger . . . ooooooooh. Rafe! Rafe! I'm *healthy,* goddammit. It's normal, goddammit. I'll . . . mmmmmmmmmmnh! I'll call Jehú. Hi! Whatcha doin'. . . . But I can't . . . what's he doing *now?* JEHU! If Daddy knew . . . but Dad doesn't know. I mean, Dad doesn't even understand that I. . . . what I . . . need. Want.

"Teddy Bradshaw! That shit! What went wrong? And Sidney. Sid . . . dear, dear Sid, that poor, miserable cock-sucking son-of-a-bitch. I promised. But Hap Bayliss! Jesus! Hap-fucking-Bayliss . . . Daddy *had* to know . . . ummmmmmmmmmmnhnh!

"I . . . love . . . you. Rafe. I love you, you son-of-a-bitch. Do you understand that? Mexican bastard. And Jehú, too. Because. Because *you* were first, Jehú. Remember? Remember Dan Dodson's house? You were the only Mexican there. . . . "Who is that Mex with S. J.?" *My* Mex, and none of your goddam business Bonita Shotwell. Bonnie Ess, you miserable prick! *You* took Rafe to bed! *And* Jehú! "Who *is* that Mex with S. J.?" I'm not a shit. I'm something. And you . . . ooooooooooooooh, My God!......You, Bonnie Ess, you're the shit . . . ummmmmmmmmmmmm. I can't breathe. . . . "Who *is* that Mex with S. J.?"

"They showed you, didn't they? The Mexican cousins fucking

in tandem. 'Jehú! Jehú! Why doesn't he call me, Jehú?' Here let me kiss . . . Why doesn't Rafe answer the phone?"

"I hate him, Jehú; your cousin's a......ooooooooohhhhh!

"What was that? Fuck the maids . . . Daddy does . . . and Uncle B . . . Of *course* he tried . . . he . . . ooohhh. Jesus!"

12

"Oh, Jesus............no............no............Christ! Oh my God; look at that! My God, Rusty! You, Rafe! Look at that! Look at *that,* you guys! My God! Those poor bastards don't have a chance! Jesus! Rafe . . . Rafe, let 'em go!"

"What are you talking?"

"Tell him, Rusty. Tell him to let 'em go. Rafe! Don't shell the Ridge! Please!"

"Please? What's wrong with you? We've got to."

"Why, Rafe? Why do we *have* to shell 'em?"

"Because it's *them,* Ned."

"They're dead, Rafe! Look at 'em: dead and dying. Rusty! Talk to him, Rusty!"

"What the hell's wrong with you? Get away from that goddam phone, Ned! Rusty, take those binocs away from him. . . ."

"Rusty . . . Rusty, *you* call Hatalski; tell him we got 'em all. . . . Call him, Rusty."

"I can't do that."

"Why? Why not? Jesus!"

13

"Jehú—straight out, okay?—like always, right? Jehú, you're just not cut out for political office. I mean, well, you're just . . . well, hell, I'm not either, goddammit. But! We need somebody in there, okay?

"What I mean is, there's a total of seven commissioners in the court, you know, and we got the five cinched, but when Cutchie McLemore retires, we'll be down to four again; oh, it's enough, but it's too close: we like it at *five*. It looks better, see?

"Now, we'd like to have two Mexicanos in the Court 'stead of the one we got now, you understand, but I can't see *you* in there. Can you?"

"No."

"Well, neither can I, Jehú. . . . Up to six months ago, I thought maybe you could; I really did. Ha! I even told old Freddie Cooke you would, too. . . . And I meant it, Jehú."

"I know you did."

"Do you, kid? . . . I mean, do . . . here, let me see what you got there. . . . No, don't go . . . Jehú, we're not through yet. Go on, close the door, will you? Take a seat; no, not that one over there, goddammit. Here, sit over here.

"You still ain't married, are you?"

"No . . ."

"Well, that'll come. . . . How are things over at El Carmen?"

"All right, I guess . . ."

"You haven't been there lately, Jehú?"

"Not for a while, but Rafa and I get together, and . . . "

"You and him are pretty tight, are you? I mean, army and school, being cousins and all."

"We're close, if that's what you mean. And, we're family."

"Took you in as a kid, did they?"

"Yeah; I was only five or six then . . . but it wasn't charity, Noddy. I mean, I was already family when I went there; do you know what I mean?"

"Did you ever know Quieto? I mean, do you remember him, Jehú?"

"No, not really; not when I think about it, anyway. I was still a kid then. . . . That was close to . . . what? Twenty years, by now?"

"Just about. You understand we had nothing to do with that, right?"

"That's why I'm here . . ."

"What do you mean, Jehú?"

"I mean I wouldn't've come to work here if I thought . . ."

"Yeah?"

"If I thought that the KBC had had *anything* to do with his death, Noddy."

"I know you wouldn't. . . . Look, I don't even know what made me say what I just said. . . . Okay? Reassurance of some sort, I guess . . . I mean, my own reassurance."

"Rafa hasn't forgotten . . ."

"No, I don't imagine he has. . . . *I* knew him, Jehú; Quieto, I mean. . . . Knew Julián, too. . . . Jehú, just how well do you know the Tuero family? I'm talking about Old Benjamín and that crowd?"

"I know them pretty well, Noddy. . . . Specially Cosme and Genaro."

"By Carter's Lake?"

"By Campacuás."

"Well, yeah . . . Cam-pa-cuás; Vince Carter's daddy, old Julius Augustus himself named it Carter's Lake. . . . But that doesn't change it, does it, Jehú?"

"No . . . it's still Campacuás."

"And you say you know some of those Tueros out there, in that part of the county?"

"Sure . . . but they're pretty old, Noddy."

"Yeah, I imagine they're getting up there, all right. . . . Do you, ah, do *you* know Howard *Haskell?*"

"Well, I know who he is, sure. . . . He's got a piece of land out there, doesn't he? A neck. . . . Oh, I see where you're going now: it joins the Tuero spread over by the Carmen Ranch's Punta del Este. . . . But Haskell's not thinking of going into the land business, too, is he?"

"No; not as far as I know. . . . He's married to Berta Tuero, isn't he?"

"That's right; are the Leguizamóns in on this?"

"On what?"

"On whatever it is we're talking about."

"No."

"Okay, but I'll tell you this: the land won't come cheap, Noddy."

"What land you talking about?"

"Same one you are."

"Well, more than the land, Jehú, we want the Fredericka Cooke Institute to acquire the Haskell-Hunter Hide and Leather Company."

"The Company and the land? Together?"

"Looks like it."

"It won't come cheap, Noddy."

"You think not?"

"The Tueros don't like to sell land, Noddy . . ."

"That's a detail, Jehú."

"You think so? If you want my thinking on this, I'll tell you: it's going to cost a lot of money."

"Ben Timmens says otherwise . . ."

"Does he, now?"

"That's Gospel, Jehú."

"Haskell's company is doing very well."

"Tell you what, Jehú: you and I handle the banking, and we'll let old Ben do the lawyering. Ben says that with this one, he can get the Cooke Institute moving. . . . And listen to this: you're the one that's going to do the Board presentation. I mean, I want Junior Klail himself to hear it from you. This is your job, Jehú. You're a *banker.* You got that? We can *always* get some shit for the Commissioner's job."

"But it's the land, isn't it, Noddy?"

"What are you talking about?"

"I said—you old sumbitch—*it's the land,* isn't it?"

"Mostly . . . but there's money to be made—all around— maybe even sixty per cent of it tax free . . ."

"It's the land, Noddy."

"It's the *land,* Jehú. That land. My daddy picked citrus there as a kid of sixteen, Jehú; picked there and up and down the Valley until he died in that train accident . . . and then . . . hold on now: how'd you know it was the land?"

"I *didn't.* Till now. And, I guess it's because you and I've been working together for a year now . . . not on this, but . . ."

"Am I slipping? Is that it?"

"Not a chance, Noddy. I just looked at it this way: there's not much land there, and it doesn't go anywhere. I mean, the land's nowhere near the River. It just didn't make much sense, so I just thought it had to be the land or something special. . . . I didn't know *why* you wanted it . . . but I did see you coming."

"Did you now? Heh! Well, it's time to go to work. . . . Here, I want you to send Esther Bewley on over to the Court House to check over some of this stuff. . . . Here, give this to her and then have her stop at Klail Title on her way back; she's to pick up a closing cost estimate for the Ponder business . . ."

"What Ponder business is that?"

"Gotcha, huh? Well, we, ah, we're going to handle a piece of El Alazán that Bowly Ponder's interested in . . ."

"Esther Bewley's his niece, Noddy . . ."

"That's right . . ."

"How much is Bowly going to owe the First now?"

"Eleven seven. . . . By the way, Ben Timmens'll be here at two; get yourself free, Jehú: I want you to hear the way he's got it set up for us. Like I said: I want Junior Klail to hear you on this.

"It's a tetch complicated, Jehú, but legal, and that old I.R.S. Commissioner up in Washington ain't going to feel a thing when it goes in. . . . See you at two."

14

Jehú's office. On top of the desk: a number of previously approved loan applications awaiting a signature. Jehú, smiling, begins to sign the notes, and thinks about his own future; not at the Bank, no, *his* future. Out there, somewhere, and not what Noddy wants or expects.

What Noddy wanted and expected was what the KBC wanted and expected: a fine, young, local, church going, little league coaching boy. And, politics. And service clubs: "No, Noddy, I can't do it," he had said. And now he was proving to be a disappointment in county politics.

"Why not, Jehú, you're a natural."

"They're shits, Noddy; and as for that Mexicano you've already got there . . . well . . . not me, Noddy."

And the Ranch had got themselves another boy; an Anglo this time. And in another two years, the second Mexicano, but not Jehú Malacara. Noddy'll just have to bring in someone to work at the First. . . . He can always go to Polín Tapia to scout for him. Or the Leguizamóns. . . . Must be a thousand of 'em out there. . . .

Jehú and Noddy knew each other and, up to a point, they also understood each other; they worked well together, and Noddy saw to it that Jehú learned and learned well. For his part, Jehú was quick, and Noddy liked that. Jehú was also quick enough to see that the KBC didn't have to put it to the Mexicanos anymore; they now went after bigger game; the U.S. Treasury, for one. It wasn't the evasion of taxes; it was their avoidance. And for that they had Ben Timmens . . . Timmens and some 12 others upstairs. The Mexicano there was Bob Peñaloza: and, *he* was church going; a Kiwanian, too, and the manager of a little league team . . . and a shit, Jehú concluded.

Bob "Newman Club" Peñaloza; Jehú and Rafa had first met him at a Newman Club dance in Austin. Bob's sister was now at the S. and L. Jehú remembered her when she worked at the Veterans' Administration adviser's office a few years before. . . . What *was* her name? Enedelia? Edilia? Delia? No matter, they called her "Punkin." Cute.

At that time, Korean War G. I. Bill vets were being shunted off into boat building courses out in West Texas. Jehú, by going back to the old bank records, traced the loans and the ownership of those schools. Not surprising, the KBC was not involved directly. Ben Timmens had handled that; he'd just returned from a six year stint at Washington after a previous six up in Austin.

Ben Timmens. Married to Edith Bayliss, daughter to an old KBC veterinarian and sister to the right honorable Hapgood Bayliss (Dem. Tx.).

Yes. Ben had done time in both Austin *and* Washington. "Damn fine tax man, Jehú. The best." The Ranch could have used Ben in New York, but Ben wouldn't budge, and so the KBC used his talents *here*. Ben reminded him of don Víctor Peláez; quiet, resourceful, except that Ben didn't drink; Edith, on the other hand, made up for both.

Edith: "Remember this, Jehú, we Anglos cleared up the brush in both Belken and Dellis County; a lot of Anglo sweat there, you know."

The point was that the old Mexicanos said there was no need to clear that much land. But the Anglos disagreed: in order to sell it, the land had to be cleared. . . . And they did both. They also learned Spanish, the KBCers did.

Also, the KBC made it a practice to buy but *not* to sell; to trade, perhaps, but no selling. The first Rufus T. Klail, dead and long gone, had practiced what he preached, and so much so that it was now in their genes. Hard to prove, but there it was. . . .

Edith Timmens spoke Spanish . . . and well. Jehú had never heard Ben speak Spanish, but that meant nothing: Jehú knew that old Mexicanos, like say, don Manuel Guzmán, and Garrido and Leal, spoke English. . . . Maybe Ben did speak Spanish.

Who's this loan for? Bowly Ponder? What the hell's Noddy up to? I'll talk to Noddy before I sign this. . . . The Institute? Noddy says the Institute—The Fredericka Cooke Institute, Jehú—isn't moving. That it's time it got moving. . . . Moving. That's Noddy's word for *making money.*

"Those accounts ain't moving, Brink." And Bob Brinkman gets cracking to make them *move.* "That's an account we can *move,* Doug." And Doug Cargill sees that it does move. . . . If not, it's the Savings and Loan. So, make it move, boys, or it's the S. and L., and working there means working with Red Barth, and who needs *that?*

Fifteen to two . . . Ben'll be here in ten minutes . . . better remind Noddy: "Noddy? It's quarter till." Noddy . . . his account of his father's train accident differs from P. Galindo's telling of it. P. says Old Man Raymond was drunk and fairly well chopped up by the Nine Fifteen. . . . I wasn't even born then. . . . *One* thing's sure: he doesn't know about Sammie Jo and me . . . Ben ought to be coming in NOW. There he is. Good old Ben . . . I'll wave: "Hi, Ben." "Jehú." And we go into Noddy's office for

A Seminar:

"Okay, Ben what've you got this time?"

"It's an arrangement concerning the Institute; and we've found a way to make it move."

"Jehú, sit next to Ben here; I'll go ahead and move around. . . . Fire away, Ben."

"It's Haskell Hide and Leather, Noddy, and we've tied that piece of land you want to the tail. . . . Everyone's agreed over there, and now it's up to us."

"Okay, Ben, now you're going to have to go slow and double back at times for Jehú and me here."

"I'll believe that when I see it, you old fraud. Look at 'im, Jehú . . . he's probably got questions I haven't even dreamed of."

"Sure I do. . . . Okay, Ben, kick it."

"Here we go: Howard Haskell, his wife, and their two boys are the owners and sole principal share holders of H and H Hide and Leather: it's a closed, family-owned corporation, Jehú.

"Now, they've agreed to convey their stock—I've got those papers here—to the Institute: a tax exempt organization under the Tax Code. You with me?"

"So far."

"The Institute *liquidates* the corporation. . . . Got that? Okay. The Institute liquidates the Haskell Corporation, and transfers the assets—under a five year *lease*—to a *new* Corporation: the Hidalgo Corp., which will then be managed by Mr. Howard Haskell."

"That's liquidation, transfer of assets, and lease. And the shares?"

"That's a good question, Jehú."

"I told you, Ben; don't look to me. He's the one you got to look out for."

"Well, I just as soon watch the both of you, if you don't mind, Noddy. Okay, Jehú: Old Haskell manages Hidalgo, and the shares are then placed in the name of his attorneys; they're also Hidalgo's directors, see?"

"See why, Jehú?"

"Go ahead. And then?"

"Then it gets cute. Legal as hell, you understand, but cute. And *tight*. The same business continues under a new name with no *essential* change in-the-control-of-the-operations."

"Tell him why, Ben."

"Hildago Corp. agrees to pay 82 percent of the pretax profits to the Institute as *rent,* under the *lease.* That's rent under the lease, Jehú. Now, the Institute agrees to pay 92 percent of *this* amount to Haskell's family in payment for shares . . ."

"Held by the attorneys."

". . . held by the attorneys as directors until Haskell receives one million five, at which time, the family's interest terminates and Cooke Institute owns the complete beneficial interest as well as all legal interest in the business."

"Any stips?"

"Yes: if the remittance to Haskell and them were less than two hundred and fifty thousand every two years—or if any other provision in the agreement is violated—Haskell could recover the property."

"Fat chance."

"Well, we just had to put it there for the Government. Look good so far?"

"What about personal liability?"

"The Institute, Jehú, has no personal liability."

"In essence, Jehú, Haskell conveys the interest in the business to the Institute in return for 70 percent of the profits of the business, and the right to recover the business assets . . ."

"In the hands of . . ."

"That's right . . . in the hands of. Okay . . . the right to recover the business assets if payments fall behind schedule."

"Which can't happen."

"Unless the KBC disappears, the Bank goes under and the goddamned world as we know it disappears as well. Right, Ben?"

"One more question."

"Go ahead, Jehú."

"Why would-should-would Haskell enter into the transaction? I mean, *prior* to the sale, the family has the right to 100 percent of the corporation's income. And now, from what you tell us, *after* the sale, they'll have the right to only 72 percent of the corporation income . . . AND, if I got *that* part straight: they'll lose the business in ten years. I guess what I'm asking is: What are the advantages?"

"The first two reasons are for money, and the rest are tied for last. One advantage, Jehú, is the capital gain treatment, for a share of the business profits they receive, rather than ordinary income."

"Fifty percent?"

"Fifty percent is right and *that* at reduced rates as well. Now, because of the existing Tax Code's charitable exemption—and—the *lease* arrangements . . ."

"Yeah? The lease arrangement?"

"Yes, through the *lease* arrangement with Hidalgo Corp., the Institute *and* Hidalgo neither have to pay income tax on the earnings of the business . . ."

"Why *neither?*"

"Because Haskell receives them free of corporate taxation—subject only to personal taxation—"

"At capital gain rates."

"Exactly: at capital gain rates, 72 percent of the business earnings, see? Seventy-two percent is taxable at capital gain rates, and *then* only half of *that*. Listen: 72 percent until they're paid the entire one million and a half . . ."

"And without the sale?"

"You got it, Jehú . . . without the sale they receive only 48 percent of the business earnings, the rest would have to go to the government in corporate taxes . . . AND, the 48 percent . . ."

"Would then be subject to personal taxation at, ah, ordinary rates, right?"

"Right! In effect, Jehú, the Institute sells Haskell the use of its tax exemptions—we don't *call* it that, of course—and this enables Haskell to collect the million five from the business *quicker,* quicker than they otherwise could and to pay taxes on this amount at capital gain rates."

"And the Institute?"

"Cooke Institute receives a nominal amount of the profits while the million five is being paid off, and then the Institute receives the whole business after the debts have been paid off. It's an arrangement, Jehú, and it's legal. The Government's grant of a tax exemption is used by Cooke Institute as part of an arrangement that allows the Institute to buy a business that, in fact, cost it nothing. What's the matter?"

"What are *we* here for then? I mean, of what use are we? I'm not a lawyer."

"That's it, Jehú: you're *not* a lawyer, you're a banker. It took us a lot of time to do this, but that's why we're here, and we could devote the time. You don't have the time. . . . I'm a tax man, Jehú, not a banker."

"And everyone does . . ."

". . . what they do best."

"Well, I felt worthless for a while there; fact is, I still do."

"Don't, Jehú. I do *this,* you do that, and from what Noddy says, you do it well. Can you give it back to me now? You can use the notes."

Jehú went over the arrangement for Noddy and for Ben Timmens; by the third time, he wasn't using notes much; he stuck to the facts as Ben had given them, and when he was stopped in mid-sentence and asked a question, he'd answer from the facts with no variation.

By the Friday meeting, when he had his twenty minute presentation with the board, Jehú made it sound ridiculously easy. Later, over a beer, he found, to his surprise, that it *was* ridiculously easy: it wouldn't fool a child, of course, and yet it *was* legal; just making use of the government grant to tax exemptions. Not evading, Jehú; avoiding.

No; it wouldn't fool a child, but there it was.

15

"Rafe? Rafe, you calling Batallion?"

"Yeah . . ."

"Tell him, Rusty. Rust! Tell him not to fire anymore . . . Rusty? Tell him, please."

"Shut up, Ned . . ."

"Hat? That you? It's me, Rafe......Can you hear me?.....Yeah; on the money..........I figure they'll be there in three-four minutes ....Brom's okay; yeah....................no.........no..........he's tucked in pretty good.......What? No!.............No, no, that's okay. Sure, I'm sure.........What? Aw, it's Ned.......Yeah..........What?..........Okay, just as soon as you guys open up on Eddie Boy..........Hat? What was that? Hat? Hat? You hear me........Okay........Look, it's Henderson ......he's crying........it's the shelling, Hat..........What? Okay . . . Ned! Ned! Hat wants to talk to you........

"Hat? It's me, Ned.......................No, I...............it's just that ....that..........because......BECAUSE IT'S CRAZY, GODDAMMIT! THAT'S WHY! BECAUSE YOU SONSOFBITCHES ARE CRAZY! EVERY GODDAM ONE OF YOU, AND THAT GOES DOUBLE FOR THAT SONOFABITCH! Hat? Hat?"

"He cut you off?"

"YEAH! Yeah . . . am I crazy, Rafe? Is that it?"

"No, you're not crazy. . . ."

"There! There! There! They're shelling Eddie Boy Ridge, goddammit! Jesus Christ!"

"Get down, Ned! Down! Don't look!"

"And don't you look either, Rafe . . . put down those binocs, Rafe! Put 'em down!"

"I'm looking to see if I can spot our guys."

"I'M NOT CRAZY, GODDAMMIT!"

"Settle down, Neddy! There's the phone, Neddy. Get to work; get it . . ."

"Bromley? Is that you? It's me, Ned! Brom! I'm sorry, Brom . . . Brom . . . Sorry."

"Let go of the phone, Ned. Ned! The phone!............Brom! It's Rafe.......You okay?"

"Yeah.......You guys okay up there? I been calling you for a long time.........."

"Couldn't hear the ring . . . you okay?"

"Yeah, I'm okay. . . . Hey, tell Rusty there's a lot of shit we can pick up out there; I figure that in about . . ."

"Brom! Listen: Brom . . . Hat wants you to disconnect right now. Disconnect! Yeah, don't wait . . . come on up here. . . . Now! Now, Brom! You got that? Disconnect right now, and get your ass up here. . . . No fucking around now. . . . Come on, I'll keep the binocs on you. Ringing off, Brom. Disconnect, Brom!"

"He coming up?"

"He damn better; I figure they're going to start raking every goddam piece of ground around here in about fifteen minutes. . . . Rusty, you take Ned down. Now. Go on, take him to Batallion."

"When you coming down?"

"Just as soon as Brom gets here . . ."

"You sure? You need anything?"

"No; look, Rusty, get Ned the hell away from here. They're going to start shelling . . ."

"Rafe . . ."

"I'll be right behind you . . . just as soon as Brom gets here."

"I'm sorry, Rafe . . ."

"It's okay, Neddy; you and Rusty go on down to Batallion."

"Is Brom coming?"

"Yeah. . . . Go on, now . . ."

16

"Thank you, Noddy, that's quite a report you've got there."

"This'll give us a start, don't you think?"

"Yes, it does, I think it also sets a direction for us, and now, with Freddie's death, that leaves the three of us. Ibby?"

"Blanton's out, for my money; and the same goes for Sanford. I think we ought to dip down to the youngsters; Sammie . . ."

"Hm . . ."

"S'right, Noddy; Sammie Jo and Jim and Arkie, too. All three. At once."

"What's the matter, Noddy?"

"I don't *know* about Sammie Jo, but I think it's high time for Mr. Jameson Agard Cooke to take over some part of this corporation."

"Amen."

"Second . . . what about Arkie, Noddy; what do you think?"

"He's ready; been ready. I think he and Jim'll do right well."

"But you're not sure about Sammie Jo?"

"Well, she *is* my baby girl and all, but . . . Oh, hell, let's go on and make her a part of the board; we'll give her Freddie's title."

"Ibby?"

"Fine with me."

"And the boys?"

"Should we call 'em in right now?"

"Are they at the KBC?"

"More'n likely . . . Junior?"

"Why don't we have a Family dinner first?"

"Formal and all?"

"That's right. Ibby?"

"I think Junior's right, Noddy; you know, a general announcement or something like that . . ."

"Yeah, that sounds good to me, too; and how about a *baile* later on? You know, we get Tony Peña and the boys."

"I don't see why not; we can do it on a Sunday, you know; the Family dinner and the other things."

"What do you say to that, Junior?"

"I'd rather not. Let's have the Family together; no one else. Then, later on, say a week or so, we'll make the announcement and then we'll have Noddy's dance."

"Suits me."

"We'll do it that way, then. I think the kids'll work out. Now, what are we going to do about George Markham?"

"What about old Choche?"

"Noddy's talking about his retirement, Ibby."

"Is that . . . Is it really?"

"Sixty-five; sixty-five last April, wasn't it?"

"March, and as Noddy says, we need to think on this."

"Won't the state of Texas take care of him?"

"Of course it will, but I'd like for us to take care of him, too."

"Has Noddy come up with something that I don't know about?"

"Well, I've been thinking that old George's no rancher, and he sure as hell's no cowboy either, but he knows our vaqueros; speaks the language—their langauge—and he's been Mr. Markham to them as long I can remember."

"And?"

"Well, I figure he can drive a pickup here and there, drink some coffee, be handy from time to time, you know."

"Ha! That's what the old sumbitch's been doing for years."

"I think Noddy's got something else in mind, Ibby."

"I do, and here it is: we give him an office here at the Bank, upstairs somewhere, and he'll be in charge of bank security. When elections come round, or whenever we need him, he'll be around. Like I said, handy."

"The Leguizamóns could use him too, couldn't they?"

"They sure could."

"Well, have you talked to Javier about this? . . .I don't think Javier'll put up a fight, I'm just asking to see if anyone's checked, is all."

"Old George is pretty loyal, you know."

"No argument there, and nineteen fifty nine or not, he's a *rinche,* and he doesn't take shit from anyone."

"But I'm not talking about a gun, Ibby. Junior?"

"We're not either; just taking care of one of our own."

"Well . . . I guess I was thinking about the Mora affair."

"Ambrosio Mora was drunk; he was disorderly, he was disturbing the peace, he was abusive . . ."

"Hold on, Nod: you sound just like Augie Van Meers did on the stand. All I said was that it'd be better for George, if George did not carry a gun; that's all."

"Well, he will, you know."

"I guess it's not that important, you all. Point is, we can use him, and we'll just take him on. . . . By the way, Noddy, how is his wife* doing?"

"She been sick?"

"No, she's fine, as far as I know; I guess he and Santos have been married, what? Thirty? Thirty-five years now?"

"We're all getting old, Noddy . . . it's closer to forty or forty-one by now. And Billy?"

"From what I hear, he's still rocking along over there."

"Okay, this brings us to the Escobar boy. Again. How's he doing? You go first, Ibby."

"He's okay; he's a bit of a bull shitter at times, and I'm not too sure that the girls like him all that much, but he does his job."

"Such as it is. I don't want him, Junior: we'll keep him right where he is, and then we run him for Commissioner, just like we said."

"Bit slow, is he? Well, we didn't ask for much anyway . . ."

"A couple of years down the road, we're going to have to promote him with a title change. We'll think of something. Anything else?"

"It'll keep."

"What's that Noddy?"

"It's about next year's county and federal elections. Nineteen sixty'll be here before we know it. Hap's going out, there'll be a change here and there . . . should we bring the kids in on this?"

"No, there's no need for them to get involved, at this time."

"Okay. Now, if you'll just open the Osuna files . . . no—the other one, Junior. The yellow ones. Got it? Looks like we're home free on that one . . ."

*Santos Maldonado. Her twin sister, Ciriaca, was also married to an Anglo: a remarkably dull and dependable man who operated a chain of tire stores for the KBC in Houston, William Barrett and Dallas. The Maldonados had been Ranch Mexicans with a difference: they didn't live there; could, then, no longer be considered Ranch Mexicans. Were not, then, true Ranch Mexicans.

Echevarría had known their father, Efraín Maldonado, when Efraín was fifty-years-old; *something* had happened at the KBC and Efraín had quit. "Walked on out; walked out and never said a word." And that had been some thirty years ago; he'd been a cowboy, and that's all he knew. As it turned out, he went to work for Celso Villalón as a goatherd.

A month later, he showed up at the east Ranch gate and told Nate Blackburn: "I've come for my stuff, Nate; it's inside. What's it going to be? Do you go on in and get it for me, or do I go in and pick it up myself?"

Echevarría says that Nate Blackburn opened the gate and let Efraín into the property. On his way out, he stopped at the gate again and walked on over to Nate, and said, in Spanish, this time: "Ya sabes, Neit, cuando se te ofrezca." It was an offer: an offer of friendship, an offer of service. They each rolled a cigarette; this was followed by a handshake as Nate called out—in Spanish— "Efra . . . te cuidas." Take care, he had said, and with that Nate walked to the fence and kicked it as hard as he could as Efraín Maldonado walked away: a KBC Mexican no longer or ever again.

The Witnesses

17

O. E. Patterson   D.o.b. 11 Sep 1896   m. Jane (Tuttle)   1 Son

Yessir, people can talk all they want to, but there's no escaping the fact that the Leguizamóns are fine, upstanding Christian Americans; and they are patriotic, to boot, and they're not afraid to show it.

They came to the Valley like a lot of people did right after the Civil War; they're Old Spanish, you know: directly from Metsico. They put their shoulders to the wheel from the very start. They're hard-working and reliable people, and they picked up the language pronto and not like some who, right now, in Nineteen Fifty-nine, mind you, still don't speak a word of English. And, if some of them *do,* then it's a secret because I sure as hell don't hear it much during election times or whenever I see or mess with them. But the Leguizamóns are something else: they are in-dus-tri-ous . . . and there's no denying that 'cause it's a fact. Oh, I know some Valley Mexicans bad mouth 'em, but that's just plain old *envidia;* sure it is: you see, they just don't know how to work together, but, I'll tell you, that sure as hell doesn't make 'em independent, either. Damndest thing you've ever seen, isn't it?

But the Leguizamóns! Fair's fair and Mexicans or not, you've got to give them credit. Why, I heard one of them—I don't rightly recall the name offhand—but anyway, I heard one of them, oh, I know who it was: young Ira Escobar—his mother's a Leguizamón from Jonesville—anyway, I heard that boy give a talk on what it meant to be an American, and believe me, he brought the house down. Old Colonel Vandergriff was almost in tears, and he's an Army man; know what I mean? A real man. Of course, Ira went up to A and M and then on to St. Mary's; for my money, there's no two better schools in the state of Texas. No sir; you can keep your Baylors and your Rices—and we all *know* about Austin. Anyhow, Ira spoke on what it means to be an American, and he talked about his great great grandfather and his dream about this country and all. I tell you, whenever some of those ingrates stand up—and that's the word—why, it makes your blood boil. Colonel Van says that a couple of years in the service'd fix them—I don't know but what he may be right............Service's probably too good for 'em, although some of them *have* gone in. I know for a fact that the boy at the Bank's been in the Army according to Noddy; I don't know the boy to speak to him, but he doesn't look friendly. Ira's different; he's a Leguizamón, and they were aristocrats in Metsico, don't you know. But aristocrats or not, when they crossed that Rio Grande, they came to work and will you look at 'em now? That's what this country's all about; if you work hard, you earn what you get. Every penny.

And what I said about *envidia* still goes; they call the Leguizamóns all sort of things and names. Behind their backs, too, 'cause those Leguizamóns are tough hombres; let me tell you. And they're not *pushy*. No sir. When Antonia Leguizamón married to the first Jimmy Cooke way back there, it was a matter of money to me, but there was a lot of love, too. And they was proud of their Spanish blood, and now Jimmy Three's got a quarter of Spanish in him. That's why he's got that temper, see. I guess that that makes Ira and Jimmy Three some sort of relation; like a fourth cousin or something . . . but the Leguizamóns don't throw *that* to anybody's face: they don't have to. . . . Proud but *good,* y'understand?

And Old Javier? Seventy if he's a day and going strong. Damn good businessman, too. Started off as a ranch hand for the Tuero family over by Campacuás, he did. And now? Well, he's got some of that land there, too. And let me tell you *this:* he was a hell raiser in his day. Something like his older brother . . . Alex? Alejandro . . . that was it. . . . Anyway, Javier was a hell raiser but a hard worker, and I'm talking about some forty-five years ago when he mixed it up with Manuel Guzmán . . . yeah, that old man. Wasn't old then, of course, and we was all working there together. . . . Yeah, Old Manuel didn't like what Javier said, and waited until Javier got off one of the broncs there . . . Manuel walked over and whacked him to the side of the face. . . . Javier'd gotten up, but Manuel told him he'd crack his skull for him with the quirt head; and he'd done it, too. . . . They didn't cross a word for twenty-five years either; but the Leguizamóns are real people, and Javier is the one who went to see Manuel. Personally. Even offered his hand. Quality folks, like I said. Look, what can you do with someone who behaves like a gentleman? Ira's the same way, I hear: won't let himself be insulted; he'll brush it off, just like that. Takes a real man to do that, don't you think. They're fine people.

18

"Henderson!"
"Edmund D.!"
"Pardue!"
"Benjamin T.!"
"Dada!"
"Francis J.!"

"That's it, Frank."
"BATR-RY!"
"Platoon! 'toon! 'oon!"

"AT — EEZE!   Rest!"

"How about you, Greek? What are you going to do; where you gonna go?"

"Tokyo first and second; I'm going to walk into Hanako's House and *never* come out; fucking M.P.s won't go in there, anyway. How 'bout you two? Rusty?"

"I was planning to go with Rafe, but . . ."

"Look, he'll be in that hospital three weeks sure; by that time, we'll all be back here or up on the line, one. Ned?"

"I'm going to Tokyo, Greek. First week anyway . . . then down to Nara. . . . You guys ever go to that bath house on Yomuri? By the big white house with the garden right on the sidewalk? They've got some good ass there . . ."

"There's ass all over that fucking island. Right, Rusty?"

"Ass is ass and it's good anywhere . . . want to go together, Greek?"

"One question: how much money you got?"

"What? What are you talking about?"

"You better leave some of it here, Farmer Brown."

"What are you talking about? I got four months pay . . ."

"That's right, and you could take a year's pay and still blow it. Keep some here."

"Lay off, Greek; he's old enough . . ."

"You want to come with me, Rust? Yes or no, and that's it. If you do, you leave two months pay here. You got a choice. Ned? You coming?"

"Hey, Greek, I'll leave one month's pay, okay?"

"Two."

"Two......okay."

"Leave it with Dumas, no sense blowing all of it in two weeks. Ned?"

"Yeah, I'll go to Tokyo with you guys, but then I'll go to Nara, like I said. I don't want to see one familiar face my last week there. Not one. I'll be seeing you guys back here soon enough . . ."

"Hey! Anybody for Kobe? Osaka?"

"Hardy!"

"Yoh!"

"Kobe, okay?"

"You got a deal."

"Osaka?"

"Yoh!"

"Who's that?"

"Me . . . Mosqueda . . ."

"Okay, Jake . . ."

"Keep it down . . . here comes Bracken."

"Oh, shit!"

"BATR — RY!"

"Platoon, 'toon! 'oon!"

"TEN — CHUT!"

"All the men present or accounted for, Sir!"

"Who's still laid up?"

"Buenrostro, Riley, and Taggart, Sir."

"Is the transportation ready, Sergeant?"

"Yessir."

"I want to say a few words to the men."

"Yessir. AT — EEZE!"

(What the shit! Fuck-off, Bracken! You popeyed-son-of-a-bitch! You know what you're doing Cap'n? You're screwing up my screwing time in Tokyo, goddammit! A few words? A *few* well-chosen words, is it? Yeah? Well, I got your well-chosen words hanging right here . . . take a bite, a hike and a kite, you fucker!)

"Men, (up your ass, you Texas son-of-a-bitch!) take care of

yourselves on this R and R. (Spin it, shit head!) We don't want any cases of V.D. when you get back. (Yeah? Well, Curly, my 'only's' got the clap so we're playing burn out . . . shit brain) Take care of yourselves (Morning-noon-and-night, Fuck Face) and remember that the uniform you wear (It's coming off for good, Shit Hook!) is that of the United States Army (No shit, Little Beaver?) so wear it proudly (I got your *proudly* here, Limber Dick). That's it: have a good time, and we'll see you in a couple of weeks.

"Dismiss the men, Sergeant."

"I'd like to say a few words to the men, sir."

"Don't keep 'em too long." (Shove off, Barge Ass)

"BATR — RY!"

"Platoon! 'toon! 'oon!"

"TEN — CHUT!   AT — EEZE! Now: those of you who want to leave some money here, pass it on to Corporal Dumas . . . and get a receipt! The trucks are ready, and we leave at 1430 sharp; you got two hours for chow and to get ready. The APA shoves off at 1630; you're late and you stay! Now: I'll be at Mama Yoshi's the first week; it had damn well better be an emergency, and of the first goddam order. If it is, I'm available. The second week I'll be in the Boso Peninsula, so if you need me, go to the Golden Paradise, and ask for Three-Hole Annie!"

"WAY TO GO, HAT!"

"At ease! Corporal Frazier'll be at the Paradise the second week. And I guarantee you that that too better be an emergency. Mama Yoshi for Week One and the Paradise for Week Two. BATR — RY!"

"Platoon! 'toon! 'oon!"

"TEN — CHUT!"

"Dis—fucking—missed!"

BANZAI BABY, YOU WATCH YOUR ASS!

19

Earl Bennet   D.o.b. 13 June 1889   m. Sarah Watfell   2 Sons

The trouble with Mexicans is that if we give 'em a raise, they'll either get lazy or they'll quit on you; just like that. Looky here: they make as much as they want, and if we step in and give them some more, why, they'll just blow it away. You know, they 'git drunk' and play them rancheras on that juke box there and adiós mi dinero, boys. And that's no lie: I know what I'm talking about.

I *know* Mexicans; I was raised here, see, and I know 'em. I know *exactly* what's on their minds, and I know what I'm talking about. You baby 'em too much, and they'll ree-sent it; you're damn tootin' they will.

Hell, I know what I'm talking about. You ask 'em how they're doing, and they'll smile and say, 'Poco, poco.' And you know they don't *need* much and really, they don't *want* much. They're not spoiled like we are. . . . And smart? They ain't nothing on this land they don't know about. . . . And loyal? No question, boy. But, and it's a big *but:* don't you cross 'em. Ever. 'Cause they don't forget. You cross 'em once, and that's it . . . I ought to know: I was born here . . . raised with them, don't you know.

Here, let me tell you this: you know Marcos Esparza? Those big old red-heads over by the River? Okay . . . now, they're not Ranch Mexicans, never have been . . . but they all get together once in a while, you know: in their bailes and such. Well! About twenty-thirty years, just south of Bascom, by the Mex cemetery?, they was having themselves a baile *and* a barbacoa; you know. Beer. Meat. And Music. Like Old George Markham says . . . yeah, beer, meat, and music . . . anyway, one of them Esparza boys is having himself a dance with one of the Buentello girls—and you know the Buentellos is *old* . . . older'n than the Santoscoys . . . than the Paredes, even. See? Anyways, that old boy is dancing and giving a grito now and then—you know how they are—when all of a whoop the music stops, sudden like, and a voice ring out in Tex-Mex: "Hey cabrones, Esparza, you just let go that there Rancherita," or something like that. *You* know. And he . . . what? No, not in English; in

Mexican. Well, I mean to tell you that that there was no nigger church there. It. Got. Quiet. And believe this, if old man Klail himself hadn't happened to be passing by those houses there, why those Mex would've cut each other to pieces. Right there and right then.

You know the reason old Rufus T. stopped? He got suspicious. It was too quiet. Good thing he stopped, too. . . . Why, old Rufus T. walked right in there and, in the middle of the dust and everything, see, he yells: "Qué pasa, amigos? This is a baile; familias presente. Hear?" *That* quieted them down all right . . . they wasn't going to be no fight that night. It was the timber of the Klail voice that did it, don't you know. And the women were grateful. Ain't nobody. More grateful. Than Mexican ladies. No siree, they ain't. But whatever it was, ever since then, the Esparzas and the Buentellos have had bad blood between them.

"That's the way they are. Work like hell, you know, but don't give 'em too much—money or liquor—or they go sour on you, sure as shootin'; I know them; hell, I was raised here.

I know what I'm talking about.

20

"Hello, Frank . . ."

"Hi-ya doin', Stupid?"

"Well, doctor, I'm doing all right, but my elbow still hurts everytime I take a pee. . . . Aside from that . . . how are the rest of the guys, Hat?"

"Getting ready to go on R and R. I'm baby sittin' for a week over at Mama's............You stupid shit, you got no business being alive, you know that?......What you did was stupid. You didn't have to do that . . . you had no goddam business. Aw, shit: I knew you were dumb the first time I saw you at Sill......Goddam concussion alone would've killed anyone with half a brain. . . . Well?"

"I like you too, Frank."

"Yeah, well . . . you almost made Bracken happy."

"Yeah; we Texans do got to stick together . . . hey, speaking of which . . ."

"Joey's fine . . . he's not going on R and R."

"Why not, Frank? What' the matter?"

"It's Joey . . . he, ah, he found Charlie's name on a casualty roster . . ."

"What?"

"Charlie's buried here, Rafe . . . about nine miles, over at the Provisional. . . . I'll see about some transportation . . ."

"Can we go, Frank? Joey and me?"

"Damn right! I'll get you guys a jeep, but I *could* get you a goddamned staff car . . ."

"Ha! If anybody could . . ."

"If anybody could, Hook Frazier could."

"Yeah . . . how's he doing? Is he okay?"

"Yeah, sure. . . . He'll baby sit the second week. You'd never guess where."

"The Red Cross."

"Close enough. Hey, I gotta go; check with Fats at the motor pool . . ."

"You still got Aldama out there?"

"Sumbitch is going to do eighty fuckin' years in this man's

army, and then he'll still only have three years of good time . . ."

"You're a soft touch, Frank."

"Yes, I am. . . . Sure, I am. . . . Stupid, you take care. Remember: if you do stick a nurse, pick an ugly one, they're loyal."

"Thanks, Frank . . ."

"Yeah......See ya............Rafe!"

"Yeah, Frank!"

"Get well, *cabrón!*"

"Yeah. . . ."

21

George Markham D.o.b. Unknown m. Santos Maldonado 1 Son

Mexicans! What the hell do they know? Why, if it hadn't-a-been for *me,* they'd all been rounded up for sure. Damfools. . . . First thing they see is this circled star of mine, and right away: Pinche rinche! Well, I'll pinchy-rinchy them, goddammit. I'm their *friend.* What the hell do *they* know. . . . Why, I married a Mex, didn't I? And then they call me prejudiced. Well, I don't give a good goddam *what* they say. I know I'm *not,* and when I up and shot Ambrosio Mora it was in the line. Yessir. It was something that couldn't be avoided; and he wasn't as drunk as they say neither. Man was dangerous. He was agressive, and loud too. Shit: where the hell did he get that liquor anyhow? It was an election day, goddammit, so he jus' went across that River and got him some *pisto.* Sumbitch had a knife, too; I just know he did. Hell, they all do. They don't change.

Bunch-a goddam ingrates.

22

Johnnie Pike.   D.o.b. 23 March 1909   m. to Ralph Pike
No children

Lived here all my life: Klail born and Klail raised; probably die here, too. (Laughs) Traded with Mexicans all my life, and got three of them working for us: there's Lucio over there who's been with us forty years; he goes back to the time my daddy opened up; and there's Andy Pumarejo who works on the books and waits up front, and then there's Faustino there in back; he's the stockboy. They're good workers, all of them, and they all speak English, too. Andy's got one year in Klail Business School already. . . .

Times've changed and for the better in many ways. . . . Here, let me tell you this: now, you know Vicente Vizcarra, Jr., he's got Seamon Loans and the V. V. Used car lot, and the insurance, right? Well, when his old man started, he had nothing. I mean nothing, a-tall. . . . And, when all of a sudden he bought that brand new car . . . I'm talking about a long time ago, now . . . and money was hard to get then . . . I mean the government wasn't cranking it out like it is these days, know what I mean? Okay . . . now, where did Vicente Vizcarra—the old man—get enough money to plunk down six hundred and ninety-five dollars, spot cash, mind you, for a brand new Plymouth? 'Cause that's what he did: dollar for dollar. Went up to Heck Barth's and from one to six ninety five, al contado, too. No credit, no sir.

Times've sure changed . . . why, it's nothing now for any old boy to buy himself a car, any type of car, too. . . . But then? Ha! Know what happened? Ol' Walt Dembro took one of his deputies— T. J. Moore, I think it was—yeah . . . and they went over to see Vicente, you see. Vicente had rented himself a little office . . . with a telephone in it, too. . . . He had rented an office on the second floor of the Texas Theater; right smack in the middle of Anglo town. It was a small office, but big enough for Vicente . . . first Mex in that part of town, too. . . . Walt wanted to know *where* he got the money. Probably *how*, too. . . . And that was a damfool thing to do, I agree; Vicente was a hard worker, don't you know. It was just that it was a lot of money in those days, see . . .? And since he couldn't, I mean, he didn't-a, didn't have a bank account, at the First, well, anyway . . . you could see Walt's point of view. . . . Know what I mean? Vicente didn't get riled or anything. Had no grounds, either; it was the Depression and that was a lot of money . . . and . . . and . . . know what I mean? Anyhow, Vicente explained that he was an employee for a Houston insurance company: that's right, Houston, way up there. One of those ten-cent a week things. Well, old Vicente had all Mexican town sewed up; he'd been at it for four years ol' Walt come to find out. He did, old Vicente did. He had had an office over on Third . . . by the park? And when his company rep came down, he told Vicente to get himself a better office. A nicer one. The Company did the paper work and the contract was sent from up there in Houston, and a month later, Vicente had moved in. Caused a slight commotion, and he did have a leetle trouble getting himself a phone at first. . . . But look at him now, and look at his boy; the boy's not the man his father was, but he does all right. Makes no le hace to Vicente Jr.; he gets along.

Those were hard times—for all of us—Anglo, too, you know. I mean, we were just as poor as anybody. And some Anglos were new here, but they stuck it out. One thing: the Mexican people didn't go much for the Relief; too proud, they said. That may be, but you got to be practical, too. If you need it, take it. After all, it was a government thing. I mean, it was all right. . . . Not like now, though; this is different, and the damn government's into everything, don't you know. Everything.

Look at our camera shop: three full time employees, and you ought to see the paper work. But even with that, it's better'n it was before. The Mexicans are better off, too, don't you think?

23

". . . And are you from Houston, Buenrostro?"

"No, sir; I'm from the Valley."

"Oh, yeah? What town?"

"Klail . . . Klail City."

"Where's that?"

"Well, sir, that's about forty miles west of Jonesville."

"Oh, yeah . . . is that by Ruffing, then?"

"No, sir . . . we're south of Ruffing."

"South? Are you on the River?"

"Yessir, right on it . . ."

"I always thought you were a city boy . . ."

"Yessir."

"I understand this is your second time around."

"Yessir."

"You planning to make the Army a career?"

"No, sir."

"Hatalski thinks you're good Army material, and what he says and thinks is usually pretty good enough for me . . ."

"Yessir . . ."

"He, ah, says, that, you, ah, y-you did a fine thing; you've got five witnesses . . . that's probably three more than you need . . . Lt. Brodkey is one of them . . ."

"Yessir . . ."

"The Heart goes with the, ah, the g-gash . . . and, ah, Lt. Brodkey'll do the paper work for the Bronze . . . it's a V . . . that's for Valor, Buenrostro. . . . I'll, ah, I'll go ahead and sign it. You, ah, you've got me . . . in your corner . . ."

"Yessir . . ."

"Well, ha! how are they treating you? Okay?"

"Yessir."

"And, ah, how's the food? The chow?"

"Well, sir . . ."

"Yes? What is it?"

"It's all right, sir . . . it's Army chow, sir . . ."

"You miss your own food, right? I mean, ah, you, ah, miss that good Mexican food, eh?............Ah, you'll be out of here before you know it. . . . Don't forget, we owe you an R and R. . . . Just report back, and let us know when you're ready."

"Yessir; thank you, sir."

"Not at all, Buenrostro. . . . Good luck, and we'll see you soon."

"Yessir."

24

Kaz Kocurek   D.o.b. 7 March 1914   m. Mary C. Kocurek
Six children

I'm an independent tire dealer, and I wouldn't have it any other way. When you work for yourself, you've only got yourself to answer to or to worry about. Work for yourself; that's the only way.

We're from Pittsburgh, my wife and I . . . East Liberty, really, but then you've probably never heard of it. And we're Polish. In the Valley, we're Anglos . . . few niggers they got here, are Anglos, too, looks like. And, we're Catholic, my wife and I.

Came here after the War; my sister-in-law married one of the Ponders from Bascom . . . you probably heard of them. . . . We came down in March of Forty-Seven for a visit, and then came back in August to stay. For good that time: all six of our kids were born here and baptized over to St. Ann's. Got two of my boys working for me here.

I started in batteries and kept that as I moved on to the tire business; got my loan from Noddy Perkins himself. He's a good man, and he appreciates a hard worker; I do too. I've got four full-time employees in the shop and one on the road up and down the Valley. You probably know him, he's around your age.

When we first came down, to stay, we didn't know much . . . like anything else, I guess. We went to St. Luke's to mass our first Sunday, and it was in Spanish. *That* was a surprise. Went to mass there for three or four Sundays in a row until we settled down and joined St. Ann's; it's in our part of town. Closer. I don't go along with having two Knights of Columbus's clubs, but that's the way they do things here . . . that's what I was told, and that's what I've found out since.

Mexicans don't bother me. I mean, their being Mexican doesn't bother me. We call them Spanish back home. Back home . . . I guess that'll always be home to me. . . . Yeah, the Spanish. But here they're Mexicans, and they're proud of it. They should be, I guess; I'm Polish and I'm proud *of* it, but as I said, down here we're Anglos. You know Fidencio Parra, the one they call Four-eyes? Fidencio says I'm an Anglo. Fidencio says that in Belken County, that in the state of Texas, really, it doesn't matter what you are: if you ain't Mexican, then you're an Anglo. I guess that's why I said what I did about the colored. . . .

The Church means a lot to me and my wife; we're, ah, we're what you'd call parish oriented, you know? Down here it's different, different from 'up North' as they say here. Oh, we've got get-togethers and all of that, but it's not the same. The Mexicans are the same way as the Anglos in that . . . not quite, but somehow. They're something like us, too, in a way. Somewhat. Like . . . like school for one; now you'd expect their kids . . . they're Catholics, see?........All of our kids went to St. Ann's up to the eighth grade and then on over to Klail High, but few Mexicans send their kids to St. Ann's . . . I mean, they don't *support* it. Well, how're you going to have good teaching those first few years. Know what I mean? There's more: but that's just an example . . . they . . . you, you know . . . they *like* to be separate.

It's not like that everywhere; you know that yourself. You're from here, right? I mean, born and bred, right? Let me tell you what I mean: going back to the Klail City thing, I'm now a member of Alhambra . . . that's the Fourth Degree . . . and when we go up to Houston or to William Barrett or on over to San Antonio, why, some of those Fourth Degree Knights are Mexican . . . like you; well, a little older, like me, but they're good folks, too, you know. And some of them are real Mexicans, you know: from across. . . .

25

"Lieutenant?"

"How are you, Rafe?"

"I'm fine, sir."

"Yeah, you're looking much better . . . better than you did a month ago. . . . I, ah, I'm sorry about Brom. . . . All of us are . . .

"You . . . all of us, all of us did what we could. . . . Is there *anything* I can do for you?"

"No, sir . . . but, ah, I want the lieutenant to know I appreciate it . . ."

"What's that? I haven't done anything; not yet, anyway."

"I mean, coming over, sir. I appreciate it. . . . Hook . . . Frazier . . . came by earlier."

"Frank had already told you about Charlie Villalón?"

"That was some time ago, sir."

"Well, maybe I *can* do something; is there anything you need?"

"Frank's going to help on that, sir . . . that end of it, anyway. But . . . could you find out how much longer I'm going to have to be kept here? I think that I could rest at base camp just as well. . . ."

"Has Captain Bracken been here?"

"Yessir; he was here again. Around noon . . ."

"I thought so. . . . Mind if I pull up a chair?"

"No, sir."

"Thanks. . . . Rafe, I'm going to say something, something that Frank Hatalski doesn't know . . . probably doesn't have to know or need to know. Frank's Regular Army, Rafe; this is his life. . . . No, no let me go on. . . . Ted Bracken wanted to court-martial you. . . . Wait . . . he wanted a court-martial for exposing the unit . . . that's what he said; the unit, for exposing the unit to danger. . . . At first, he blew his stack 'cause Rusty Pardue—and not you—brought Henderson in . . . I *know*, Rafe, I know . . . Henderson cracked up and Rusty was on the verge . . . in fact, Rusty thought you were dead, and he reported as much. Bracken quieted down after that, but, when Frazier brought you guys in . . . you didn't know that? Yeah, it was Frazier. . . . Anyway, when Frazier brought you in,

Brom was already dead . . . he was probably dead when you carried him . . . or dying, Rafe . . . there wasn't anything you could do . . . there wasn't anything anyone could do . . . at that point. . . . Well, when you turned up . . . Bracken blew his stack again. . . . He said that the Battery's position was zeroed in . . . that we were goners— that's what he said—and then, that it was your *fault*. Every bit of it . . . Frank doesn't know, Rafe. . . . We're all getting out, and Hatalski has to stay and live with Bracken and the Army. . . . At any rate, Bracken called one of the new firing officers—his name's Bill Waller—you *know* him . . .? Bill followed Ted Bracken into the CP tent . . . I was there. . . . Andy Lawson came right in after us, and the two enlisted men cleared out; it was pretty bad, Rafe. . . . Waller said some things . . . by this time, you were on your way to the aid station and later on Hatalski drove you here. . . . Anyway, Bill Waller said he was recommending you for the Bronze Star. . . . This on top of Bracken making an ass of himself. That took the wind out of Ted, but then he thought Billy was bluffing, and that's when he tried to pull rank on him . . . I don't know why, but that's Bracken's way. . . . Waller then looked at me, and I said I had you spotted on the binocs. And I had. Andy Lawson did too. Later on, we found out that several of the men did too. . . . So, there you have it. It's a good medal, Rafe. . . . Nothing cheap about it. . . . And you know Bracken . . . he got over it as if nothing had happened, but half the Battery heard him; anyway, Frank's bound to find out, but he hasn't as yet anyway. . . . I'm going to write up the commendation. . . ."

"Jesus."

"There's more, but that's about it . . ."

"Doesn't he *know* why I *had* to get Bromley away from there? Hasn't he . . ."

"Rafe!"

"Sorry, Sir."

"Don't *sir* me, Rafe . . . "

"Well . . . hasn't he learned by now that the Chinks are going to fire back? They're damned good, Lieutenant . . . I mean, we had two-three hundred of our guys out there. That . . . that son-of-a-bitch . . . I don't *want* his goddam medal . . ."

"It isn't his, Rafe . . . it's not even his to give . . ."

"How . . . how's Ned? Henderson?"

"He looks all right . . . but you think he's had it?"

"I think so . . . he looked pretty bad up there. . . . And Bracken's wrong about Rusty Pardue . . . Rusty's a kid . . . a baby, almost . . . but he believes. . . .

84

"Yeah; it's funny . . . he believes in people . . .and now . . ."

"Yes?"

"Well, I may not say it right, but he believes in himself . . .and *I* believe in him . . . he's had a *rough* life, everyday of his life it seems. But he's good. . . . Where is he now?"

"I guess he's getting off the Adams by now; it was due in at 1000 . . ."

"Did he go with Dada? Dada's a good man . . ."

"Rafe? I've got to go now . . . I'll come by next week. "

"Better make it early . . ."

"Oh, why is that?"

"You're supposed to find out when I get out of here. Remember?"

"I'll work on it. . . . You're sure you want to get out?"

"Yessir. . . . Thanks a lot."

"I'll be back."

26

John F. Goodman   D.o.b. 16 Aug 1885   Widower   No children
Sgt. Maj. 12th Cav, U.S. Army (Ret.)

I'm seventy-four years old, so I imagine that that makes me some ten, maybe eleven years older than George Markham. Is that about right? I first met him in Nineteen Fifteen during the troubles here in the Valley; I was in the First Cav then. We came to the Valley in August of Fourteen; a year later, I rehitched for another six at Jones, and that's when I saw my first aeroplane; that was in Nineteen Fifteen here in the Valley; met George then, too. He was younger than I was, and I thought much too young to be a Ranger, but he was a Ranger, all right. . . . He must have been twenty or twenty-one then, you know, and that's when he married Santos Maldonado.

There was Texas Guard units with us, and we had everything: engineers, signal corps, ambulance companies, *field* artillery, infantry, of course, truck companies, pack trains, baker companies; you name it. Everything, don't you know. We came loaded for bear 'cause those were harsh times on both sides of the River.

First off, I was in the First Squadron Virginia Cav, and then I was put on the Second Squadron Colorado Cav. We had two Harry Smiths then, Major Harry D., Commanding the Field and Staff, and Captain Harry F. of Troop A, New Hampshire. My C.O. was Johnny McQuillen: a mean so-and-so . . . no good.

We did mostly patrol work. There was some danger to it, and some of the boys was roughed up and died, but the Mexicans paid for it; I don't mean you no offense, but that's the way it was during those times.

So, we had the Army, the Texas Guard units, and the Rangers. The Rangers raised hell . . . and they murdered people . . . that's the word, all right, and there's nothing else to call it. The Valley Mexicans did raise a stink and all, and then, a-course, there *was* that State hearing with that Mex legislator from Jonesville . . . but dead people don't come back, and never have except the Once; that legislator was not afraid to speak up, but that was one voice. . . .

One thing, though, they *did* cut the number of Texas Rangers; I don't know or even remember, but whatever the number was, they was busted down to four companies for the whole state, and I think each company had something like seventeen men. Yeah, they were broken . . . but George Markham, Mexican wife and all, hung on; he was kept on, and he's been in the Valley ever since. I can swear to *that*. He must've been born around here is all I can say, and he speaks that Tex-Mex. Yes, he does. I did, too, for a while, you know; specially when I was married to my first wife. I met her in Jonesville, but she was from across: she was from Barrones, Tamaulipas. . . . But the Valley always had soldiers . . . always. All the way from Jonesville to the Arroyo del Tigre. Know where that is? I'm talking of two hundred and seventy-four miles from Jonesville to way up the River. . . . Fifty thousand men at one time, not counting the Rangers. . . . That's right.

Saw Mexican service, too; crossed in Barrones, then further up the Río to Soliseño Ranch just a few miles from the Klail City pumping station; we had troops there, too. . . . Shootouts all over the place: Toluca, ah, the old Vilches Ranch, the Buenrostros' place. . . . I also crossed over to Río Rico once; some of our boys had been swimming out there, and when they crossed to the Mex side, they were picked up there and then. Col. Parker he sent three squadrons as a show of force, and they surrendered the two boys to us. Each got six and two-thirds for that little caper o' theirs. . . . Yessir, six months in the Fort Jones hotel and then two-thirds of their pay was dee-ducted . . . they didn't get busted down a grade 'cause they were buck-ass troopers to begin with. . . .

But like I said, I've known Choche Markham a long time; a *long* time; he'ad red hair then, and what's left is sandy now. . . . And, oh, did he love to dress up; right smart, too. He used to come a-drinking with us when we'd come in to Fort Jones. We'd go on over to Fourteenth Street with all the bars and cantinas and then work on over to the City Market there; we couldn't go across, the Mexican side being PRO-scribed, you see; off-limits. . . .

The Mexicans on *this* side didn't mind the Army too much—some of them was in the Service, too—but it was the Texas Rangers they looked to, and the Rangers walked around like the big muckety-mucks. . . . Not saying they liked the Army, no, but the Rinches rankled, y'understand? We were Regular Army, too, so we had to set an example . . . besides, I had made up my mind to do my thirty right here in the Valley if I could . . . and I did, for the most part; I started in Forty-One—the year of the War?—with thirty, close to thirty-one years in, see? And let me tell you this: had no more than six months bad time in all. Not bad for a boy from Roanoke, Virginia; that's where I was born.... I couldn't retire just then, but I finally got out in Forty-Four with thirty-four under my belt. . . .

But George was something; even then. We knew what *they* were up to by scaring the Mexicans on both sides, but all it got 'em was some dead on their side and a *montón* . . . a good number?, yeah, a *montón* of Mexicans on this side. *Bulto* ain't the same as a *montón,* right? But, you see, they also killed Mexicans from the *other* side of the Rio Grande. Even then . . . even then . . . I *thought* George was angling for something, even then. You know, I always thought he worked for the Klails, and Blanchards, the Cookes, and for the Leguizamóns, too. Even back then . . . and now, too, right?

'Course, I never saw George in any *real* action; I only heard about it . . . like the time when them two Mexican deputies from Relámpago got into their car with the two Mexican prisoners and then some eighteen miles on the way to Klail, the car was stopped, and the prisoners were strung up. Markham said his Captain gave a receipt to the Mexican deputies for the two prisoners. . . . I don't know about the receipts and that might be Choche's imagination working again, but the car *was* stopped and the two Mexicans *were* hung then and there . . . as for the deputies, I knew 'em; still do. . . . The Rangers took their *guns* away right then. . . .

But it was in and around Klail here that a lot of shooting was done . . . at the canal head gates, over by the pumping plant and station, places like that. But it was just hit and run stuff; like at the head gates in Klail, that lasted two or three days and nights . . . días y noches, see . . . I'm not excusing the Army, no sir, but the Rangers started a lot of stuff, too. The Army paid back, like the time—I remember now—like the time some ten days before the trouble at the head gates in Klail . . . it was over by the El Galvestón Ranch . . . near the River road, but on this side . . . it's got another name now . . . anyway, some of our troopers were ambushed; one killed and two wounded. We *arrested* five Mexicans living at the Galvestón, and we turned them over to the deputy sheriff, and he jailed 'em. That night, the deputy sheriff took three of them and started on the Ruffing road. . . . That deputy was, ah . . . what *was* that man's name? Magee? . . . McGraw? No, but it's close. . . . Don't let me wander off, now . . . Maharg! That was it . . . Maharg. There's still some of them Mahargs left right there in Jonesville, I'll warrant. . . . The upshot is that the next morning we found the three Mexicans dead; been executed, see? But it wasn't *us; we* turned *them* over to the civilian authorities. . . . Later on, they come to find out that they were ranch hands and not raiders, a-tall. . . . Now, Choche *used* to say he had been in on that in Nineteen Fifteen, but *now* he says that he wasn't. There's a lot of stuff that he now says he wasn't mixed up in . . . it's the same old song, don't you know? I mean, I've *heard,* heard mind you . . . that that boy . . . Ambrose Mora? The one he shot in Forty-six by the J. C. Penney Store? In Flora? Well, the Flora Mexicans say that Ambrose was the nephew of *one* of the three Mexicans Choche shot in Nineteen Fifteen. . . . Wouldn't surprise me in the least . . . and that shouldn't be too hard to investigate, should it . . . ?

Do you know Martin Holland? He's not a Mexican, you know. He was here, rather he was up at Ringgold Barracks, and *then* Fort Jones by the time I got here in Fourteen. Martin's been here ever since Nineteen Ten or so, see? Married a Mexican like I did, and he went native; I mean, by Nineteen Fifteen, he was speaking Spanish or Mex, but pretty good. And fast, too. He'd served with Old Man Taggard at Ringgold, and from *there* to Fort Jones when Colonel Parker took over. . . . Parker married a Mexican woman, too; a rich one, see? Anyway, Martin was in a Field Hospital unit and *then* in the Cav with me. And remember Leland Bass? He worked for the Buenrostros, and he was a good friend to Echevarría. Well, Leland was born in Indy-Anna, he was . . . but you'd never know it. . . . Old Echevarría now, he's got *me* by a dozen years sure . . . thirteen probably; yeah. Yeah, I'd say thirteen was more like it. . . . Anyway, Martin Holland's the one to ask . . . if you can get him to speak English. Ha! Oh, he ain't forgot none . . . he just likes the Spanish . . . probably tell it better in Spanish, too. . . . Now; *he* knows Choche Markham. Doesn't like him, but he *knows* him . . . they're sort of concuños, too. That's right. Martin's married to Sofía Anzaldúa, and *she* is a first cousin to Santos and Ciriaca Maldonado. How 'bout that? Yeah, it does go back, doesn't it? Hmph! Old Efraín Maldonado . . . that's Choche Markham's father-in-law. Efra doesn't exactly brag about his Anglo sons-in-law. . . . Do you know Wallace Hengston? The tire man? Wallace Hengston is one of the dumbest white men in the North American continent. Yeah . . . old Santos and Ciriaca must be sixty years old, if they're a day . . . and their Daddy's eighty-six or seven. . . . He's of Echevarría's *camada* more or less. . . . Well, as I was saying, you get a-hold of Martin Holland; be worth your while.

27

Thelma Ann Watling   D.o.b. 25 December 1899   m. M. Jacob
Watling   Twin girls.

They are the kindest people on earth you would ever want to
know; hard working, long suffering and loyal as anything. And
their babies are precious with those big, black eyes. And I would
judge them as dependable, too. Elodia is a case in point; she's
married now, but she came to us when she was thirteen or so and
stayed with us for over ten years; then her sister, Ana María, came
to us, and she worked for another ten or twelve years; and now it's
Claudia, and she's been here the longest; going on fifteen years
now. Why, they all saw the twins grow up from kindy to high school
and college and now Betsy has a boy and a girl of her own and
Dorothy's expecting again.

The Macías girls all turned out well; Jake knew old Rosendo
when he first managed Grogan's packing shed. Jake hired him on
the spot. Rosendo's not a Valley Mexican, you know. I think he
crossed when so many of them did in Nineteen Twenty or so, and he
settled here in Klail. Rosendo was very religious; Pentecostal, I
think; at any rate, they call each other Brother, Sister, *you* know.

I remember when Jake and I used to drive out to deliver citrus
baskets to them and bring along home-made candy and popcorn
balls and pecans; they were really grateful. Appreciative, don't you
know. And they could show it, too. Jake, he'd drive up to the side of
the house, open up the trunk and take out one of the baskets. And
then, he would walk it to Rosendo's front door. Personally; I mean
he wouldn't let Rosendo carry it at all; Jake was like that. I'd stay
in the car and wave at the girls; prettiest things you've ever seen
and now Elodia and Ana María are both married and living in
Chicago, of all places. Can you imagine?

28

"All set?"

"Just about; here, give me a hand with this . . ."

"Got it?"

"Yeeeeeep. Here, Hook . . . there . . ."

"Rafe? Hook?"

"Yeah?"

"That jeep ready? Come on, hurry it up."

"Okay, okay."

"Come on, take off."

"What's with Frank?"

"Aw, he's getting R. A. in his old age . . ."

"Red Ass?"

"Regular Army, *cabrón.*"

"What does *that* mean? You and Joey and Sonny are *always* saying that . . . and now you got Frank doing it too. . . ."

"Aw, it's just a word . . . it doesn't mean anything . . ."

"Yes it does; what's it mean?"

"Well, sometimes it means ass hole; in a nice way. . . . You know . . ."

"In a nice way . . . like Louie Dodge?"

"Yeah, but Louie was a poor *cabrón,* he. . . . Wonder where he is now? You think they kicked his ass out?"

"Rafe, the goddam Army's not about to waste anything. . . . He's doing something somewhere."

"Ho! Would you trust him with a knife? In the kitchen?"

"I wouldn't trust *you* with anything anywhere. As for Dodge, well, he was already nuts when he *got* here. . . . You ever notice how Bracken used to baby that old son-of-a-bitch?"

"Naw . . . Old Dodge . . . he sure liked to talk on the phone, though."

"I *told* you he was a crazy son-of-a-bitch. . . . Hey, looky yonder: that guy's throwing up. . . . Boy, when Frank said 'baby sit' he meant 'baby sit'. . . . Who's supposed to be in charge of this trash?"

"Some guy named Leonard."

"You know him, Rafe?"

"Nope . . . must be from the stockade; that's where they got these guys from. . . . Boy, that's some work detail over there. . . ."

"Bunch of fuck-ups is what they are. . . . But that's what they get for fuckin' up: picking up the goddam dead. . . . It's a shit job, either way. . . . Hey, make for that bunch over there . . . watch your step, there's a lot of shit here. . . ."

"Hi . . .

"I said, 'Hi!'"

"The man said 'Hi,' goddammit, where's Leonard?"

"He's over there."

"Over *where*, Fuck-up?"

"Who you . . ."

"Shut up, Fuck-up . . . I asked you a *question*: Where is he?"

"He's over there . . . the tall one."

"He's over there, *Corporal*; you got that?"

"Corporal . . ."

"That's right, goddammit. Corporal, you Fuck-up! . . . Go on, Rafe . . . I hate these fuck-off sonsabitches. Well, they're getting theirs: picking up the goddam, fucking dead. . . ."

"Wonder what they write home about?"

"Those fuckers can't write . . . they weren't worth a shit on the outside, and they're not worth a shit here. . . ."

"Why're you leaning on 'em?"

"*You* should, too, Rafe; it's shit like that that can get you killed. . . . . Ha! But now they're learning a trade . . . yeah . . . maybe they'll all be embalmers and undertakers when they get home. . . . Yeah, one good thing about Fuck-ups, *somebody's* got to pick up the dead. . . ."

"Yeah. . . ."

"That must be Leonard. . . . Pull over."

"Leonard?"

"Yeah? Oh, yeah! How you guys doin'?"

"Pretty good. I'm Frazier; Hook."

"Yeah, sure . . . glad to know you."

"This here's Rafe . . ."

"The spotter? Yeah, I heard of you. . . . Just get here?"

"Yeah . . . what do you need first off?"

"Where shall I begin . . . begin at the beginning, the King said, gravely . . . Lewis Carroll? . . . Oh, well. Let's go sit over there and away from this shit. . . . By the way, how many points you guys got?"

"Sixty-four; Rafe here's got seventy-three . . ."

"Ninety-six, and *I'm* still here . . ."

"You a Regular? On this detail?"

"I was a captain in World War Two."

"What happened?"

"There were a lot of captains in World War Two . . . I'm a Tech now, but it's R.A., and when I retire, it's going to be the highest grade held: Captain's pay."

"You got a Warrant for that Tech?"

"Damn tootin'. You guys A.U.S.?"

"All the way . . ."

"I *like* the Army . . . this is a shit detail, but *someone's* got to do it. . . . Half the prisoners here are Regulars . . . the other half's A.U.S.. . . . They've done worse things."

"Worse than this?"

"Worse. Curious?"

"Not really. . . . Rafe?"

"I got all I can handle watching this shit . . ."

"Weren't you up on the hill; with the binocs?"

"Yeah . . ."

"Remember the guys putting the bodies in? Well, sometimes they gotta take 'em out . . ."

"Shit . . ."

"That's the least of it . . . but it's all relative, boys. Now then, there's a hundred and twenty head count here. How many guards you guys got?"

"Rafe?"

"Twenty . . ."

"Rookies?"

"Every damn one . . ."

"Shit . . . but that's the way it goes, I guess. . . . You guys got anything else up there . . . besides beer?"

"That's it . . . Blue Ribbon . . ."

"These guys don't give a shit *what* it is. . . . Ah, this is how we usually work it out: the place's already roped off; your guards'll stand two and be off four. There'll be eight guys on and eight guys off with four supernumeraries . . . in case anyone gets sick . . ."

"And they will."

"And they will, right. The four'll take over in that case and so on. . . . Now then, the Battle Police should be getting here around six. Sharp. Our guys get up at four, and that's rain, shine, shit or snow. They do close order drill from four-thirty to five. . . . They eat from five to five-thirty. At six, I blow the whistle, and it's off to work we go. . . . The body pick up begins then and goes on to chow time. . . . Chow's from . . ."

"These guys eat?"

"You'd be surprised . . ."

"I just saw one puking out there, and he's not even working . . ."

"He'll get used to it. . . . Chow's from one to two . . . and then the work goes on till four thirty; then, more close order drill, then chow. We put 'em to bed at seven."

"What does the Battle Police do?"

"Not very goddam much. . . . *Their* shit job is to search these shits; they're all thieves; the B.P.s and prisoners both, I mean. There's a lot of fuckin' money and other shit here . . . valuables, you know. . . . The B.P.s shake them down. . . . They're pretty good; other B.P.s then shake *them* down—officers! Major Stang says he wants an 85 percent recovery. . . ."

"How do you figure that?"

"It's done. . . . Anyway, Major Stang'll show up two days from now . . ."

"There's going to be two days of this shit?"

"Three, counting today's. . . . It's a big job, Hook. . . . You pray for rain and cooler weather; your rookie guards are going to need all the help they can get. Oh, yeah: if they're up to it, they're free to shoot. One more stiff won't matter . . ."

"Bull shit . . ."

"Yeah, I'm just shittin' . . ."

"Who's Major Stang?"

"Graves Registration . . . Finance Corps . . . name it. He's in charge here. Our guys won't be any trouble. . . . It's bad, but it'll work out . . . it always has. . . . Just tell *your* guys not to look too much: I'm serious. And *now,* let's go get that beer. . . . How much you got?"

"A couple a-trucks full."

"Good; we'll set up a beer brigade. That's right . . . you got to work 'em 'cause they're sonsabitches, but you gotta pay 'em, too."

"No argument there, Leonard."

"Name's Chuck, Hook. . . . Come on, I want you guys to meet the pushers . . ."

"Just a minute."

"What?"

"Leonard?"

"It's Chuck, Rafe. Remember?"

94

"Do you know me?"

"Do I, Rafe?"

"I think you *do* . . ."

"Hey, you two, what's up? Rafe?"

"I don't know, but about . . . well, just about a little over a year ago, I think it was, I was on a pole detail; we were fishing guys out of the river. . . . It was me . . . Harkness, Blair, Reese, Olivares . . ."

"Which Olivares? Pippo?"

"Yeah . . . what about it, Leonard?"

"Chuck . . . you're right . . ."

"But that wasn't your name then. What was it?"

"Fairbanks . . ."

"It sure the hell was . . . and *you* were a Master Sergeant."

"What the hell's this all about?"

" I don't know, Hook. . . . Are you C.I.D., Chuck?"

"Yes, I am. . . . Here . . . pass it on. . . . Can I have it back? Thanks . . ."

"And then what was all that shit about you being a captain in World War Two?"

"I was, Hook; I'm also a lieutenant colonel—temporary. My Regular Army rank's that of captain. . . . You're pretty good, kid."

"No, I'm not. . . . Are we supposed to 'sir' you now?"

"No. And that's an order. It's Chuck; all the way."

"What the hell. Is this shit. All about?"

"Thievery; large scale looting of dead bodies . . ."

"What do you guys expect? You're using thieves to begin with . . ."

"Not all, Hook . . . some of the shit happens to be C.I.D. . . . We think it's the B.P.s . . . here, at Provisional, and someplace else: we don't know exactly *where*. . . . Did you really recognize me?"

"I thought I did. How'd you know I was on binocs?"

"Oh, I picked up some stuff here and there . . . just enough. What'd you see?"

"I saw the stuff being put in bags, that's all."

"Yeah; we know it's the bags; trouble is, they don't all go where they're supposed to . . ."

"Umph."

"Right. . . . Come on . . . let's go see the pushers."

"What was the pole detail, and where was I?"

"Oh, we were fishing bodies out . . . Frank was with us, you were still laid up."

"My foot, right? I remember now . . ."

"Anyway, Chuck here was in charge of that detail . . ."

"That's right. . . . We've got a good number of them pegged

already, and there'll be some more here tomorrow . . ."

"C. I. D. . . . I'll be damned."

"That's how it is, Hook. Those are the pushers there."

"Do they know, Chuck?"

"They don't suspect a thing . . ."

"Yeah, but now we know . . ."

"So what? You guys are clean. . . . It'll be over in a week or two, anyway. Come on . . ."

"Fuck-ups."

29

Rebecca Ruth Verser   D.o.b. 12 Oct 1912   widowed: Bart Verser
1 daughter

The main thing *I* don't like about Mexicans—young or old, it doesn't matter—is the way they look at you. Brazen. I warned you that I am a frank person. They see you coming: they look at you. You walk past them: they look at you. I know *what* they're looking at, they are looking at my legs! I'd pull their eyes out, if I could. They're horrible; I wouldn't have them working for me for anything. And inside the house? Are you kidding? Never. No sir. The way they look at you . . .

My father came to the Valley in the Twenties, and he said they were worse then. Worse than niggers, he said. Worse is what he said because they didn't know their place. . . . They weren't uppity, you know . . . they just wouldn't go away . . . they were *always* around. And speaking Spanish; all the time. It's enough to . . . oh, I don't know. . . . And Lord knows what goes on in those, those, those *cantinas* of theirs; I can imagine. And that music! It. Goes. On. And. On. All night long. The louder, the better.

And don't tell *me* they don't speak any English, because . . . Well, *I* am not going to learn any Spanish just to please them. . . . I didn't need it as a girl, and I don't need it now. You won't hear *me* struggling with that kitchen Spanish . . . it isn't even Spanish, is it? Not the real Spanish anyway. It's one they made up. My Ellie was a Spanish minor at San Marcos, and she should know . . . she says they speak a dialect, and *that* doesn't make it real Spanish, don't you see. It's a dialect. And they all speak it . . . even that boy at the bank, the one who taught high school with Ellie for a while. . . . He taught *English* there . . . you know the one . . . the one Noddy hired at the Bank. Oh, I can't hit on his name just now.

Anyway, if they like Spanish so much, why don't they go to Mexico? It's right there. It's right *there,* right on top of us, for crying out loud. . . . In *my* day, the Mexicans didn't go to school with us; in Ruffing, for example, they went only as far as the fifth . . . any higher, and they had to come here, to Klail, and *how* they got here

97

was their business.

And I'm not saying they're *all* like that . . . don't get me wrong. But you know what I mean . . . it, it . . . it gets to you after a while; it gets to *me*. My God! I've walked into the Kresge's-and-what-all, in and out for fifty years; and the girls? They *still* speak Spanish. Oh, they'll speak English to you all right, but just as soon as they're through waiting on you: there they go, right back at it again. . . . It's bad manners is what it is. And you think *they* care? And now? Now, they go on to school and even graduate sometimes, but they still go in that Tex-Mex of theirs. . . . Thank goodness there are some educated ones finally. . . .

You ought to hear Ellie and her stories . . . but she's a good girl, and no Mexican can complain about Ellie showing favoritism; not Ellie. She's tough, but firm, just like I was when I taught there.

30

"Rafe, you remember the time ole Ned blew up? You know, when the Chinks? At Eddie Boy Ridge?"

"Sure . . . I remember . . ."

"You know *why* he blew up, Rafe? You know *why* he went crazy?"

"Why?"

"'Cause he talked a lot. Well, I talk a lot, too, but I mean he talked a lot to himself. And that's not right. He heard voices; he told me so. You can go crazy that way, and that's why he blew up. . . . Don't you know about those things?"

"You hungry?"

"What?"

"Are you hungry?"

"No!"

"I wish I had a candy bar; one of those goddam Snickers; you remember them?"

"You went to college, didn't you?"

"Just the one year."

"Well, I didn't finish high school, but I read about that kind of stuff. . . . Talkin' about Ned. We had a good school there in Elton. Elton, Louisiana, yessir . . . I went as far as the tenth grade; well, *up* to the tenth grade . . . that's pretty good, right? I mean, that, that's being a sophomore. Right?"

"Right. Call in, Rusty."

"What?"

"Call in. Batallion."

"Right. Right."

"There. . . . You remember when we caught the Chinks there, at Eddie Boy Ridge?"

"Sure I do."

"I wadn't angry at 'em, you know."

"What do you mean?"

"Well, I, I don't *hate* 'em; I used to hate 'em. A lot. But not anymore."

"Why not?"

"I don't know . . . I just *don't*. Now, *last* year, when they caught us in the Pass? And, they, ah, they put it to us?"

"Yeah?"

"Well, I really did then, boy; I really hated 'em then. . . . I really did: they're shootin', and it was cold, and we were caught there. Like rats, you know. Just like rats, and, boy . . . I really did. I *hated* their ass. Man, they . . . why, shit, I'd-a-killed one of them if I'd-a'seen 'im . . . I would've, boy, right there. Boom! You know? Bring in the guns, yeah! But . . . I don't know now. I don't mean I don't *hate* 'em, you know, but they're not my friends, right? And, and that's why we're here and that's why they're over there on that other hill..........but......but, ah, I don't know, it's funny."

"Yeah . . ."

"Remember that time?"

"Sure . . ."

"Boy, that was a long time ago, right? Eddie Boy Ridge? How many yards is that, Rafe? I mean, how long ago . . .was it?"

"Well . . . about seven months, I guess. Eight."

"Let's see . . . well, we can work it out. . . . Yeah, ole Ned. He was a nice old guy. . . . I wonder where he's at?"

"Probably home."

"Yeah . . . he got out on one of them Section Eights or on one of them Section Nines. Boy, I sure don't want one of them. . . . I want to go *home,* but I want to go home *right*. Know what I mean? Be somebody when I get home. I don't want nobody to go around pointing their *goddam* finger at me..................How about you, Rafe?"

"Yeah, I want to go home, too......."

"You okay, Rafe?"

"Yeah, I'm just tired . . ."

"What are you going to do when you get home, Rafe?"

"I don't know; I'm just going to go home for a while, but I want to get out of here first."

"Well, *I* want to get out of here first, too, you know . . . I, I . . . we're not home safe, I know, but . . . but, I don't think we're going to get it. Shit, we've been through too much, right? Remember? We were in the Pass........'Course, Charlie died, but . . . Hey, those are nice guys, right? Those are good friends you got. I got friends like that, too, but they're not here, they're, they're at home, but you got friends here . . . you know. You got Joey, and, and that crazy guy, what's his name? Sonny . . . he's a case, isn't he? Ain't he a lick, though? And I sure had a good time with you guys in Japan. That was good, boy; I, I really liked that. You guys really know how to have fun. I'd never, *never,* been to a . . . to a whorehouse. Anywhere. You know; no money. But that was *good;* I liked it there, but you know, those, ah, girls . . . they're not really whores, are they?"

"Oh, they're whores all right."

"Yeah, but I always figured that they, ah, that they'd be real *old.* Those are young girls, I mean, they're, shit, they're *my* age, *your* age, right?"

"Yeah."

"Yeah. . . . Boy, I sure had a lot of fun. Did you?"

"Yeah, I had a lot of fun, too. It was good . . ."

"I did . . . I really did. . . . That was nice. That was a lot of fun. Yeah.........."

31

Edwin Dickman   D.o.b. 3 Jan 1931   m. Carol (Haley)
Three children

Jehú? Sure I do and Rafa, too; sure. And that whole bunch that came on over to Klail High from the . . . from North Ward School . . . just about that time. I remember Delia Serna and Ruby ah . . . Ruby Moreno. Delia's married to Servando; I see her at the lumber yard once in a while, and old Servando's been with Kirby Produce since high school. . . .

Jehú and Rafa and a few others went on to college after high school . . . well, not right away but after the service. I was in the Navy myself; fact is, Jehú and I were going to go on in together; volunteers, but he signed up in the Army earlier . . . and I haven't really seen him that much since . . . at least I didn't or hadn't till he got that job at the Bank . . . but we're talking a passel of years, here.

If Jehú had an Anglo friend, it must have been Bucky Paxton . . . ole Bucky shot himself . . . you remember that? He'd married that good looker from Flora . . . what *was* her name? It was on a Saturday night that he shot himself; by the levee I remember it was. . . . We still don't know why he did it. . . . Boy, his folks sure took it hard; only child and all. . . . Jehú was at the funeral; only Mexican there, too. But he and Bucky couldn't have seen each other that much after high school . . . still, the Paxtons went and got Jehú; he's a *cumplidor. Punto,* you know; won't let you down.

Now, when Penrose and I opened up the branch office over in Edgerton last year, Jehú handled that end of it for the Bank. He knows about loans. . . . Boy . . . he's a smoothie; oh, I don't mean he *acts* smart, you know; he . . . ah, he knows what to do, see. He's really done well there: name on the door and on the desk, you know. But we didn't do the business there, Jehú took us to the coffee lounge upstairs and sat on the sofa and all.

I think it was about that time that my Dad was thinking about Jehú joining the Lions, but I never did know what came of that. . . . There wouldn't have been any trouble; maybe Jehú just didn't want to, you know. I mean, Ira Escobar's a Lion, and he

hasn't been here that long . . . and, Ira's . . . TIPPY ORR! . . .
Tippy; that was her name—Bucky Paxton's wife—ah, widow.
Tippy Orr . . . yeah; sure. She was from Edgerton, and in high
school, I'd see her when we'd go to places like the Wagon there
in Edgerton or over to the Greek's place in Bascom; they were
hangouts, you know. On weekends. Tippy Orr . . . the talk was that
Marv Schilling—probably not true, 'cause you know how *he* turned
out—and played football, too. . . . Goes to show you . . . I'll tell
you who was a cutter, and that was Charlie Villalón: Anglo, Mexican, didn't make a difference; he just got after it and wouldn't
let go. . . . Anyway . . . where was I? Oh, yeah, no, old Jehú
just didn't join. As I said, he most probably didn't want to either
. . . but he was welcomed, I'll tell you that much. Ira's still there,
roaring away at every Tuesday lunch, though; and he's a hard
worker, I'll tell you. . . . Public spirited, too. Shoot, I've told him
he ought to consider going into politics any number of times.

32

"Who was Sergeant Kell, Rafe?"

"Where'd you hear his name?"

"From Hook, at chow. He said that a guy named Tomkins from Baker Battery was as fucked up as Terry Kell . . . that Kell went crazy . . . or something like that. Did you know him?"

"Yeah . . . Kell was with us at the beginning, when some of our guys got killed. . . . We had a forward observer named Cowans then . . ."

"Was Cowans an ass hole?"

"Yeah . . . he gave Kell the wrong distance and elevation. . . . Sonny Ruiz was with that group . . ."

"Our Sonny?"

"Yeah, they were laying wire that day, and Sonny was showing the guys from Signal where to lay it when he heard the one-oh-fives coming over. Sonny yelled out, but one of the guys was killed outright. . . . Two-three others died later. . . . If it hadn't been for Sonny yelling, though, it would've been worse . . . a hell of a lot worse."

"Jesus!"

"Who's this Tomkins anyway?"

"A new guy, Rafe. Hook says he knew him from before."

"Before what?"

"I don't know, Rafe . . . all Hook said was he knew him from *before,* and then he said Baker Battery was in trouble. . . . What do you think?"

"Hooker knows a lot; knows a lot of people, too. . . . But Kell wasn't to blame, Rusty. He was running the guns, they were sensing, and you've got to rely on the forward ob., you know.

"I was there. . . . Call came in to say that they were firing low and to raise the guns a click or two . . . but it was a late call. Shit, by the time Ol' Kellie raised 'em, there must've been anywhere from four to eight shells out there . . ."

"God!"

"That's right . . . but it was Cowans' fault. . . . All the way ....He was transferred out, but Terry Kell stayed here. . . . It

104

wasn't his fault, but he went ahead and killed himself anyway . . ."

"What? How?"

"He shot himself . . . we'd all gone out one night; we were in a back area at the time, and we'd each had a couple of beers . . . Sonny, Joey, Terry, and a couple of other guys. . . . Sonny and Kell were pretty close, and Sonny knew it was Cowans' fault and said so at the Inquiry. . . . Shit, *everybody* knew it was Cowans' fault. Fucking Inquiry just recommended a transfer for him, that's all."

"Who was Battery C.O. then?"

"Same one . . . Bracken . . ."

"Who did he replace?"

"It was a guy named . . . ah . . . Morton; no. Martin . . . yeah, a guy named Don Martin. He went to Regiment from here and that's when Bracken came in . . . and Bracken brought Cowans with him. . . . Bracken's an incompetent."

"What?"

"Bracken knows *shit* about artillery . . ."

"Rafe!"

"It's true, goddammit! Hey, it's time to call in, Rusty . . ."

"You sure?"

"Go on.......no. Here, let *me* do it..............."

"This is Badger Four; over."

"It's *me;* we're okay up here."

"Are you all right?"

"Yep; this is Badger Three. Out."

"Who's answering the phone, Rafe?"

"Frazier . . ."

"Is Hatalski still there?"

"Yeah . . . why?"

"Well, I heard he was coming off the line pretty soon."

"We all are . . "

"We *are?* When?"

"All of us are . . . three days from now."

"*I* didn't know that."

"We're all being changed around."

"All the teams? Why?"

"I don't know if the teams are being changed; we'll probably just work with another forward ob., that's all. We still need that third man here, though . . ."

"Did you see Ned his last day here . . . on that R and R?......Oh, you were in the hospital. . . . He really went crazy, *didn't* he; after he came back, Rafe? Rafe? Gee . . . I thought I was going crazy . . ."

"We're too dumb to go crazy. . . . Remember what Bracken

said?"

"Yeah . . ."

"He's a sorry son-of-a-bitch. Say it, Rusty. Say it!"

"He's a sorry son-of-a-bitch."

"That's right, and he's horseshit. Goddam . . . Frank, Hook, me, *you, all* of us, have saved his ass too many goddam times. . . . You listening?"

"Okay, Rafe . . . Okay..........It's kind a-quiet, isn't it?"

"Yeah; when it gets quiet, you just remember one thing: The Chinks like it quiet, too . . . unless they got a Bracken on their hands. . . . What are you looking at?"

"You..............."

"'Cause I'm blaming that ass hole, Ass Hole, Rusty! Aw, shit, what got me started on this?"

"I guess I did, Rafe. . . . I'm sorry."

"You didn't set me off . . . it's *him.* Call in!"

"Again?"

"There's some movement down there . . . straight ahead."

"Oh, Jesus . . . where?"

"Call in . . . report. I'm going to get a fix on them down there."

"Oh, shit. . . . Is it starting again?"

"Find out who those guys are, Rusty......"

"Badger Four? This is Badger Three."

"What's up?"

"We've spotted some people out here. Can you identify? We're getting a fix on 'em now."

"Hold on.......................Rust?"

"Yeah?"

"Call you right back."

"Okay............Rafe, they're working on it. . . . See anything else?"

"Nope............"

"Rafe?"

"What?"

"You're being transferred out, aren't you? That's it, isn't it?"

"There's the phone, Rusty. Get it."

"Shit."

33

"Calling Mr. Buenrostro! Telephone for Mr. Buenrostro."

"Here, boy, I'll take it in my office. . . . Bartender, give this man a beer, and put it on my tab."

"Thank you, sir. Oh, my! Imported beer, and all the way from the States, too. . . ."

"Yeah? Who's this?"

"Rafa?"

"Who's this? Sonny?............Joe?"

"Yeah, buddy, ¿qué-the-hell-tal?"

"Drinkin'. . . ."

"So I hear. . . . But, besides drinking, what are you guys doin' out there?"

"Serious drinkin'."

"Sounds like you're doing all right for yourself . . ."

"Fucking-A."

"When you leaving?"

"¿Qué?"

"Que ¿cuándo te vas?"

"Oh; next week sometime . . ."

"¿Cuándo?"

"It's a Thursday or a Friday. No sé."

"Where to, cabrón?"

"The Fightin' Five-oh-six!"

"Oh, yeah? Why is that?"

"Well, they need someone who can read and write over there."

"At that there place, you mean?"

"You got it, Tex. . . . ¿Qué estás haciendo?"

"We're fixin' to go on reserve status."

"You guys going on reserve?"

"Yessir . . . Rafe?"

"Yeah?"

"Hey, I'm coming by next week."

"No need to, Joe. I'll be back in a couple of weeks."

"No; I'll come by. Is Wednesday okay?"

"Sí; h'mbre . . . vente."

"Actually, I'd like to come over now 'cause it looks like you guys started up ahead of time . . ."

"This here's just the basic training, Joey. . . . How *you* doin'?"

"Ya sabes. . . . You think you gonna have enough beer?"

"Son, we got enough beer here to go into the business . . ."

"Bien haya, chingao. . . . Ho, Rafe! Who's there with you?"

"Let's see: Frank. Hook. Mosqueda . . ."

"Mosqueda? And how *is* old Jacob?"

"Who gives a shit?"

"You got *my* vote. . . . ¿Dónde está Bracken?"

"Oh, chingando la verga some goddam place . . ."

"The man's a *talent,* Rafe."

"Virtually untapped, you might say."

"But you're doing okay, ¿verdad que sí?"

"Yep! Hey!"

"¿Qué?"

"I'm going out tomorrow . . . be out for . . . vamos a ver . . . *two* days; I'll be back . . . Tuesday night. 'Ta bueno?"

"And I'll be there Wednesday . . . early."

"Sí; déjate venir que's polka . . ."

"Hey, Rafe! Say hello to the guys . . ."

"'Ta bueno, buddy . . . Joey? Joseph?"

"Sí?"

"See you Wednesday. . . ."

"Hell, yes. See ya!"

"Eso, chingao. . . . This is Badger Fuckin' Four. Out!"

"Are you through with your call, Mr. Buenrostro?"

"Certainly. Here you are my good man: A U.S. Army Issue, One-A-One Telephone, field; I trust you know what you can *do* with it. . . ."

"Who was that, Rafe?"

"Joey Vee, himself. The one and only . . ."

"He comin' over?"

"Wednesday. . . . He says he'll be here next Wednesday. . . . Hooker! Drinks all around and have one yourself. . . ."

"You're a generous son-of-a-bitch, Rafe Buenrostro."

"Another family trait, bartender. Hey, who's got a cigarette?"

108

34

Abel Manzano   D.o.b. 3 Mar 1882   m. Susana (Leyva)   3 Children

FROM THE SPANISH:

Do I have to swear? No?

All right, my name is Abel Manzano; I was born in Eighteen Eighty-Two, and God willing, I'll be seventy-eight next year, on the third of March. I was born in Campacuás Ranch; what they call Carter's Lake. I was born there, and I was married there, but I now live here in Klail with my youngest daughter, Leonor, and her husband, Gustavo Buentello; he's not a Ranch Buentello. These Buentellos are from Relámpago Ranch, the old Malacara property by El Carmen Ranch near where the old Klail City pumping plant used to be.

Yes, Esteban Echevarría is a good friend of mine, and I have known him to be an honest man; I also know he used to be a hard drinker, but he stopped drinking more than forty years ago; it's been a long time anyway. He has known Choche Markham . . . he has known *everybody* for a long time. I was born in Eighty-two, and I think Echevarría was born in Eighteen Seventy-two or thereabouts; it was just a few years after the Americans fought between themselves; in their own war.

One of Echevarría's uncles, Crisóstomo Longoria—he died in Nineteen Thirty-three—fought for the Confederates; another uncle, Malaquías Lozano fought for the United States; this one died in Nineteen Nineteen as a result of the Spanish influenza which swept the Valley at that time. They were both uncles of Esteban's; their mothers were both Echevarrías, great aunts of Don Hilarión, Esteban's father. I knew Don Hilarión; he was short and stocky not like Esteban. Don Hilarión received forty acres of his own from the Buenrostro family. This land was from the grants.

That property is near the pumping station by El Carmen Ranch where the Texas Rangers shot the three Naranjo brothers in 1915. In cold blood. At night. And in the back. I was the same age as Jesus Christ then, and I found them where they were left: on the

Buenrostro property; the Buenrostros were blameless, and they had nothing to do with that. They were left there until I cut them down. With this. Look.

It was the Rangers who took them from the deputies, and it was the Rangers who executed them. I have heard *now* and for the last twenty years, that Choche Markham had nothing to do with the shooting; I remember that from then, the year Fifteen, until yesterday, as we say, he always claimed credit for that.... That it is now inconvenient is something else.

I am not saying that that is the reason he murdered Mora's son right after World War II, but I *am* saying, and I am saying it *now, right now,* that Choche Markham was one of the seven Texas Rangers who took the Galvestón Ranch hands from the Relámpago jail; they were going to Ruffing, but they never got there; listen to this:

> En el camino a esa ciudad mentada
> En un domingo por la noche con nubarrón
> Estos rinches texanos de la chingada
> Mataron a más mexicanos del Galvestón*

But it doesn't matter what Markham says; what he says now; what he says in the future. His talking then gave him security perhaps satisfaction. That he denies it now doesn't make it more or less—*no le hace*—I remember, and I don't invent: his wife, Santos, left him for a long time, and she didn't move from her father's home until Markham came for here; hat in hand.

Yes. I covered the bodies with the tarp from my roll and took them to Santa Rita Mission—near El Carmen, by the bend of the River, and they were buried there. This cemetery I am talking about is the El Ranchito Cemetery, and it is in Esparza land.

The owners of the Galvestón Ranch were peaceful people, but after that, each man was armed until the Army and the Rangers went away; soon after *that,* the Buenrostros put dynamite on that bend of the Río Grande and the Río changed course for half a mile. The Anglos had changed the old channel years ago, and the Buenrostros just put it back to where it was.

Choche Markham knew who did it, but even with those guns of the Army, he still didn't have the . . . the *brío* to do or to say

*A literal translation of the *canción: Otra matanza, Señores* (Trans. note: in this instance, *señores* is translated as friends; the context of the song clearly shows this.) *Another Bloothbath, Friends.* "On the road to the aforementioned city (Ruffing); on a rainy Sunday night; the sonsofbitching Texas Rangers; murdered more Mexicans who worked at the Galveston Ranch."

anything. . . . It isn't important; now or then. . . . Those three young men were as dead as ever.

Now. What the Buenrostros did was to show the Rangers that it wasn't the land; it was the people that mattered.

I know Choche Markham knows this; he knows the way we feel; the way we act; and that's why he's valuable to them. With all that knowledge, he still doesn't *understand*.

One thing: don't get Esteban Echevarría started on Markham; *eso es cuento de nunca acabar* (that's a story without end).

U.S. ARMY form 1001-C.   Report, morning.   dated: 11/1/48

MORNING REPORT. DATE: 13 Sept 51. T/4 Robert L. Sherman. Battery Clerk Battery B., 219th F. A. Bn., Bracken, Theodore S., Capt. F. A., Cmd'g.

All men present/accounted for. At 1031 hours, 12 Sept 51, a rocket attack by one unit of the 15th Rocket Squadron, Chinese Communist Forces (C.C.F.) attached to the 13th Div., I Corps. 3rd Army, caused minor damage to the field facilities and firing stations.

EQUIPMENT: Kitchen, One each: Mobile, field, truck. Destroyed.

CASUALTIES: killed: Frazier, Donald M., Cpl., 34679002; Hatalski, Francis N., S/Sgt. 42766378; Vielma, Jose F., PFC., 18318634. (PFC Vielma was assigned to Battery C., 219th F.A. Bn., a unit on reserve status for the week ending 16 Sept 51. Unit has been notified.)
Wounded requiring hospitalization: Abbott, Norman A., Pvt., 14661321; Buenrostro, Rafael, Cpl., 18318633; Hentrich, Gerald M., Pvt., 44560071; Mosqueda, Jacob L., Pvt. 33699544.
Wounded to aid station: Pardue, Benjamin T., Pvt., 18319561; Perry, William E., PFC., 36858670.

Lt. Col. Hughes Evans, 219th F.A., Cmd'g., inspected damage area: 1530-1545, 12 Sept 51. Forward observers, 2d Lts. Brownfield, Richard A., and Gordon, Joseph L., reported no new activity in their sectors. Transfer order #644, cut for Cpl. R. Buenrostro, effective 14 Sept 51 is hereby rescinded pending release from Hq & Hq Hosp #14, 8th Div. Equipment rec'd: two (2) ea. A.N.V./Radios, as per B Batt Req. #1438, 6 Jul 51.   *RLS for*

/s/ *Robert L. Sherman*   /s/ *Theodore S. Bracken*
_____   _____
Robert L. Sherman, T/4   Theodore S. Bracken, Jr.
Battery Clerk   Captain   FA
Battery B., 219th FA. Bn.   Commanding